First—I want to thank my best and dearest friend, Karen Walker, who gave me ideas and read every page to help edit the book. She was always encouraging me and believing in me, and would never allow me say that I could not do this. She was always truthful with me: if she didn't like something, she would tell me why. I will always value her opinion, because I trust she would never do anything that would hurt me in any way. I will always love her.

Second—I want to thank Betsy Christian, another dear friend who read the book and loved it so much that she kept reading it to her friends. Now they all want a copy of the book. She also asked me for her own copy as I was writing it so that she could always have one of the original manuscripts. She asked that I personally sign the last page of the story so that she would always have it for her own, something special that no one else would ever have. I honored that request.

Third—I would like to thank my brother, Gary Pennington, who said he would be glad to read the book and let me know if this was something that people would want to read. Although the content is not something he would normally be interested in reading, he told me that he could not put it down. He said to let my readers know that they should not start the book at bedtime because they would not get any sleep that night. I love him for that. He gave me the responses that I was looking for.

Fourth— I want to thank my beautiful daughter, Tamara, for all of her support and encouragement. She stood by me through the whole process and even helped me write the synopsis on the back cover. I also want to thank all my friends on the Internet who have been excited about getting this story into book form.

Last, but not least—I want to thank my wonderful partner of 42 years, Marty, who always encouraged me that I could write this book. He has continually supported me in everything I have done and this is no different. I know he is proud of my accomplishments and loves me with no end. I love him with all my heart and could not have done this without his support. So a special "thank you" to him.

CHEYENNE
LOVE

SJ Pennington

Tammy,
It was great to
see you again after all
these years!

All my Best
S J Pennington `09'
AKA Sherry Prout

Cover Photography by
NPI Studios, Jason Newman
6051 Turnbridge Lane
Huber Heights, Ohio 45424
jnewman@npistudios.com

Cover Art Design by
Jenny Q. Sandrof, Art Director
Blue Heron Design Group
jennyq@bhdg.com

Editing & Layout Design by
S. Davis
sld4508@yahoo.com

Published USA by
Author One Stop
www.AuthorOneStop.com

❧ CONTENTS ❧

1. WYOMING BOUND 1
2. STAY AWHILE 7
3. REJECTION HURTS 11
4. DRIVING TO BEREA, KENTUCKY 19
5. HEAVEN ON EARTH 29
6. COMING TOGETHER 33
7. WALKER'S POND 41
8. DINNER FOR TWO 47
9. THE SEPARATION 59
10. THE BOOK 65
11. A CHANCE 69
12. THE REUNION 75
13. LOVE FOR ALWAYS 79
14. LOST LOVE 87
15. HEARTBREAK 95
16. DECEPTION 101
17. THE ACCIDENT 109
18. DECEPTION NEVER PAYS 115
19. DISCOVERY 123
20. TIME FOR TRUTH 131
21. THE SECRET 139
22. SWEET MARY 145
23. SELLING THE FARM 151
24. THE SOLUTION 161
25. HARD DECISION 169
26. THE BIG MOVE 173
27. SETTLING IN 181
28. A SISTER'S LOVE 189
29. HAPPINESS IS LOVE 197

CHAPTER ONE

WYOMING BOUND

Jamie was packing to go to Wyoming to the *Three M Ranch* to buy a stud for breeding. He was really anxious about this one because the stud horse had just won several races and was really sought after for breeding purposes. The owner of the ranch, M. Morgan, had accepted Jamie's offer of $1 million. He had not met the owner yet because their conversations had all been by email and phone calls. He was looking forward to their meeting because he sounded really interesting. He had a very deep, sexy voice on the phone and Jamie thought it might be nice if this guy turned out to be gay. But with Jamie's luck that was probably not going to be the case. He had not had a good relationship in several years. He finished packing and had his driver bring the limo around to the house to take him to the airport. Jamie didn't like all the things that were expected of him, since he was a wealthy man; but sometimes it came in handy when he didn't want to drive himself. Besides, he didn't want to put the guy out of a job.

He arrived at the airport in Cheyenne, picked up his bag and went outside to meet with his ride that M. Morgan was sending to pick him up. When he stepped outside there was a gorgeous-looking cowboy standing by a car, looking as though he was waiting for someone. Jamie hoped the cowboy was waiting for him. This man was making Jamie very much aware of his presence with his 6'2" athletic build, long, dark hair and the most beautiful, stunning blue eyes. He wore tight jeans that showed a very well-formed and muscular butt, a black shirt and black cowboy hat. Jamie could hardly contain his thoughts: *God, this man is what every man or woman would want in their bed. He is the epitome of what a man should look like!*

"Are you Jamie Walker?" The man spoke with a very sexy, deep voice. Jamie could feel a twitch in his groin that told him this could be dangerous.

"Yes, are you my ride to the ranch? I have business with the owner."

"Hop in." They drove in silence for about 14 miles out into the country. When they arrived at the ranch, Jamie was impressed by the sight of an elegant, three-story mansion which appeared at the end of the long driveway. This was not at all what he had expected. He assumed the place would be a typical horse ranch owned by a typical horse breeder. "Obviously this M. Morgan is extremely successful judging by the size of this house," Jamie thought. The man driving spoke up, pulling Jamie out of his thoughts. "Go on in and make yourself comfortable, Mr. Walker. You are expected."

Jamie went in and found himself in the largest room he had ever seen. The furniture was masculine and massive, made of richly-hued rosewood and carrying a strong, sweet aroma throughout the room. It was obvious that no woman lived here, because there were no frilly curtains or dainty decorations. This was definitely a man's house. He wondered when he was going to meet Mr. Morgan. Just as he was wondering this, the gorgeous man came into the room and walked up to him. "Would you like a beer?" the man asked.

"Sure, but can I see your boss, Mr. Morgan? I've come a long way and I need to talk with him and see the horse that I've bought. Is he not here?"

"Yes, he's here.... I am Marc Morgan."

Jamie almost lost his voice. "You are M. Morgan?" He asked, knowing he sounded ridiculous. "Why didn't you introduce yourself at the airport? Why all the mystery?"

"I'm sorry for that, but I'm not a man of many words and I was trying to size you up a little before we talked."

Jamie had to admit that this turn of events was great. *This man is Marc Morgan and he is gorgeous and it appears there is no woman in this house.* Jamie wondered if that was a good sign.

Marc called for his staff to bring Jamie and himself a beer and sandwich.

"Please have a seat. We can eat something and then we can go out and see the horse you've bought."

"When I do business with someone, I like to know a little about them." Jamie said. "Do you live here alone?" Jamie knew this was an inappropriate question, but he had this urgent need to know. This man was hard to ignore.

"No, I have a full staff living here. A cook, two maids and a man servant who also drives for me when I want him to."

Jamie noted that he did not mention a wife. This was encouraging.

"Why did you want to know this?" Marc asked.

Jamie was suddenly embarrassed that he had asked this question. "Oh, I don't know, just curious." He knew this was a stupid answer and Marc noticed it also. *What is your problem guy?...get your act together.*

Marc was now very curious about Jamie. "Is he trying to find out something else about me that he's not asking?" Marc thought with much mirth! He was now aware of how uncomfortable Jamie was becoming. Marc decided to change the subject.

"Jamie, finish up your beer and let's go out to see your horse." They walked out to the beautiful stable buildings and met the horse's groom, Keith. It was Jamie's opinion that the stables were kept as clean as the house, which confirmed to him that Marc Morgan was, indeed, very successful and no doubt worth millions. Jamie appreciated this, as he was very wealthy in his own right. Once again, he was brought out of his thoughts by Marc's voice.

"Keith — will you bring Shadow out to the exercise ring so that Mr. Walker can see what a magnificent breed he is?" As they were leaving the stable, Jamie tripped and fell into Marc. Marc caught him before he fell and held him in his arms. When Jamie looked up he met the sapphire blue eyes, and what he saw briefly was desire, he thought. *Can this be that his wish was going to come true or was this just wishful thinking? Was Marc gay?* He sure didn't seem eager to let Jamie go.

"Are you ok?" Jamie heard this very sexy voice asking him. He pulled away from Marc and gained his composure.

"Yes, thanks for saving me from making a fool of myself sprawled out in the dirt."

"My pleasure, I assure you." Marc said with a smile on his face.

"Oh my god — what a sight when he smiled," Jamie thought.

They were out in the exercise ring watching Shadow being led around for Jamie to see. Jamie was not paying much attention to the horse though, instead his mind was on the way Marc smiled at him and held him that extra second. He was so deep in thought that he did not hear Marc.

"Mr. Walker! Jamie! Are you not interested in Shadow? I can assure you that I have the appropriate certification proving his genetic quality. Have you changed your mind about buying him?"

"No, I still want him. I want you too."

"Excuse me? What did you say?"

Jamie was so embarrassed that he had said this out loud. "I meant that I want you to show me more about what Shadow has done in the last year. Do you have the races that he's won?"

"Yes, of course — what kind of a breeder do you think I am?" Marc said teasingly. He knew what Jamie had said and was not going to forget about it. *He is attracted to me, which tells me he is gay and so gorgeous.*

"Oh no...I did not mean to imply..." He stopped talking because he knew he was not making any sense.

"I'm sorry to have offended you. Please, let's close the deal and let me get on my way home. I've brought a cashier's check for the agreed upon $1 million for the horse, so let me sign the papers and I'll get out of your hair."

"Whoa!, city boy. We don't do things that fast here in Wyoming. We take our time with everything we do." Marc was playing a little with Jamie.

Jamie's first thought was, "I just bet you do — one can only hope." Luckily this time he did not say it out loud. "Well, how long will this deal take?"

"As long as it takes me to get you naked and all ready for me," Marc would have loved to have said, but instead he said. "Lets go back to the house and talk some more. I like to know the people I sell my horses to."

They walked back to the house slowly, with both in deep thought. Jamie wanted to get closer to Marc and Marc wanted to get very close to Jamie.

"What do the three Ms stand for? I noticed your ranch is called the *Three M Ranch*," Jamie asked, just to have some conversation walking back to the house.

"It's from my name, Marc Montgomery Morgan. Three Ms."

CHAPTER TWO

STAY AWHILE

When they arrived back at the house, Marc called for the cook to start supper for two. "Is steak okay with you, Jamie?"

"I can't stay for dinner...I have to get back to my farm. I have a herd of horses needing my attention and a couple of mares expecting any time. I also have a deadline for the draft of my next book, so I need to get home. Sorry! If we could complete the sale now, I can make the arrangements to ship the horse and catch the next flight home."

"Jamie, I told you that we don't do things quick here. I like to get to know who'll be taking my horses. I told you that outside. Did you think I was kidding?"

"No, I didn't think that, but I thought you understood that we need to do this faster than what you're used to because I am on a time schedule and I do need to get home." *I should get out of your presence soon before I make a complete fool of myself and attack you.* Jamie was thinking as he was sitting down to sign the papers of the sale: *God, how much more do I have to endure? He is making me a bumbling idiot!*

"Jamie, I'm sure that you can make some calls and have someone take care of things back at your...uh, farm is it? I really would like for you to stay. I was going to set up the guest room for you to stay for a few days. I want you to get to know your horse that you're paying so much money for. He is worth staying for, I assure you."

"I'm sure that you are." Jamie thought. "I'll see what I can do."

"Good. Steak okay?"

"Yes, that's fine." Jamie got on the phone and called his farm hand, Derek. He gave Derek the instructions and told him to call if the mares went into labor. Jamie had built himself a really nice home on the other side of the family pond and started raising horses. His property was still part of his Grandmother's farm, which she had left him upon her death. The house was being used by his farm hand, because it was closer to the stables than Jamie's house was. Derek told Jamie that he would call if he needed him to come home. He was a little curious as to why Jamie felt the need to call, because Jamie knew he would be handling things at home. Derek wondered what this was really about. *Oh, well, he's the boss. I'm sure he'll fill me in when he gets back.* Derek really likes Jamie but has not opened up to him about his feelings. Jamie has always been so great to him — he doesn't want to spoil their friendship by coming out to him.

Supper went without incident and the two men retired to the study. They discussed the horse, Shadow, and what he would do for Jamie as a stud. Everyone was clamoring to buy this horse for stud service because his lineage was the 'who's who' in racing circles. They also discussed how Jamie would get the horse home. The one thing they didn't discuss was the elephant that was in the room. Jamie was very nervous being around Marc and it was really putting a strain on him.

Marc started to walk across the room toward Jamie. He came right up to him and stopped. He was so close that Jamie could feel his breath on his cheek. "Jamie, why are you so anxious to get away from me? Why do I make you so nervous?"

"I think you know the answer to that, don't you? You kept me here just to see how I would react to your being this close...right?"

Marc didn't say anything. He just moved one step closer and pulled Jamie into his arms. Before Jamie could even react, Marc's lips were on his and making him respond to him. Jamie had never felt a kiss like this one. It shook him all the way to his toes. Marc pulled away, leaving Jamie feeling abandoned. He looked at Jamie and told him, "I am so sorry for that. I never should have taken these liberties with you. We just met. I'll have my manservant show you to your room. Goodnight Jamie. We'll sign all the papers in the morning so you can catch your flight home." Marc excused himself and left the study.

Jamie just stood there in the same place that Marc had just kissed him. The servant came in and told Jamie to follow him. Jamie obeyed, and when he got to his room just sat on the bed wondering what had just happened. *Why would Marc do this to me? What kind of motive would he have to treat me like this? I don't even know him.*

Jamie did not sleep very well. At one point, he thought he heard footsteps outside his bedroom door but no one knocked or came in. Somehow he knew it was Marc but obviously he decided against coming near Jamie again.

Jamie came down to breakfast and Marc was waiting for him. "I have the papers here for you and I to sign, and then my driver will take you to the airport. We'll ship Shadow to you before the week's end." Marc was being very standoffish and cool. No smiles or any sign of the man last night who practically begged him to stay the night.

Jamie signed the papers and went up to get his suitcase. He did not see Marc again before he left the ranch. All the way home on the plane, Jamie was trying to figure out what had happened. What a strange man, this Marc Morgan was. "Oh well, I'll have no reason to see him again, so get over it, Walker," he said to himself.

CHAPTER THREE

REJECTION HURTS

Jamie went directly to the pond when he got home from the airport. This was his place to think and relax. He was lying in the grass looking up at the sky, daydreaming. Derek came up to Jamie. "Hi Jamie, what was that about when you called me from Wyoming? You knew I was taking care of things here."

"I had to make it look like I needed to be at home."

"Can I ask what was so important that you needed to lie and ended up staying another day? Did the owner of the horse have a reason to keep you there?"

"Why are you asking me so many questions about it, Derek?"

Jamie sat up and looked up at Derek. Derek was fighting an internal battle trying not to tell him that he was jealous of this stranger that kept Jamie away from the farm. Derek looked so sad and Jamie noticed it. He stood up and faced Derek, "Tell me what's going on with you."

"I'm gay, and I'm so attracted to you, Jamie." The words just started pouring out. It was like a flood gate had opened up and the words would not stop coming. "I've felt like this for a very long time and I'd give anything I have if you felt just a little something for me."

Jamie stood looking at Derek as if he had not seen him before. Derek was a very attractive man with light brown hair and hazel eyes that changed colors with whatever he wore. He was 6'1" and very nicely built. That probably came from all the hard work at the farm, throwing bales of hay around. And he was standing there wanting Jamie, unlike the strange man named Marc, who basically gave him his walking papers.

"I can see that you're shocked and, if you can, please forget what I said. I don't know why this came out. I never intended you to ever know this."

"Wait, Derek — did I say that I didn't want to hear what you had to say? I'm actually glad that you told me. What would you say if I tell you that I think we should go out on a date and have dinner and some drinks? Maybe then we can see what happens."

Derek was almost speechless. "I would love to go out on a date with you. I don't care where we go."

"Okay, it is a date. Now go back to what you were doing and I'm going to the stables and saddle up a horse for a ride. I need to feel the wind on my face and clear my head."

Jamie took one of the stallions out that loved to run. That was what Jamie needed. He was running away from feelings that he needed to get over. He also thought about Derek.

Could he have a relationship with him? "I'm willing to try at least," he told himself. At least he wants me.

Marc was having a horrible day and he was angry with everyone. The servants took the blunt of his unhappiness. *Why was he doing this? A guy named Jamie? How can he have these feelings so quickly?* He had never wanted anyone like he wanted this man, and it was ridiculous because they didn't even know each other. The kiss really shook him up and made him crazy. He had to send him away before he made a fool of himself. It was all for the best. "I'll send the horse to him and that will be that." He kept trying to rationalize his actions.

Jamie was getting ready for his date with Derek. This was going to be a fun night. They would keep it light-hearted, with no strings. They would go eat and then hit some of the bars. It should be fun. Who was he kidding? It was just a way to get Marc off his mind. He knew this was so unfair to Derek, but he needed to have something to concentrate on so that he wouldn't think about Marc.

Derek came into the house looking really great. Jamie took a look at him and was taken back. He had never noticed that Derek was really a hunk. "Whoa, you look amazing!"

Derek was so happy that Jamie thought he looked hot. He tried so hard to look really great for him. He wore a medium-green shirt and tan slacks. Jamie noticed that the green shirt made his eyes a vivid green, causing him to look really dangerous and sexy. Jamie just kept staring at him. "Wow — why had I never noticed him before my trip to Cheyenne? This is going to be fun," he thought to himself. "Someone who looks like Derek tonight could definitely make me forget Mr. Marc Morgan."

Jamie went close to Derek and put his arm around him. "Let's go paint the town."

They went to dinner and then hit a gay bar. Jamie asked Derek to dance with him and he took him into his arms. Derek was in heaven, having Jamie holding him so close. He could feel his body as they moved to the music. Derek had drunk a few Margaritas and was feeling really good. Jamie was getting turned on just moving against Derek. He wanted to do a little more than dance. He could feel his dick getting hard just rubbing up against Derek. He grabbed him by the cheeks of his butt and starting grinding into him. Derek was also getting hard and wanted to be naked with Jamie and have Jamie's gorgeous mouth on his very ready cock. "Lets go home Derek. I want to show you how much you have moved me tonight."

Derek reached down and grabbed Jamie's crotch. "Moved you like this?" He then took Jamie's hand and placed it on his own hard cock, "I am *so* ready to go back to the farm with you."

As they were driving home, Derek reached over and unzipped Jamie's pants. He immediately pulled Jamie's cock out. It was very hard and thick. He bent over and took Jamie into his mouth. Jamie almost wrecked the car with that move.

"Oh my god, Derek — what are you doing?"

Derek raised up and asked, "You mean you don't know?"

"Well, yeeeeessssssssss!" Was all he could get out. Derek was already back to work. Jamie was moaning and was really having a hard time keeping the car on the road. It didn't take too long before Derek was getting rewarded for his efforts.

"God that felt good Derek. I needed that so much, you have no idea."

"There's more where that came from, if you're willing."

Jamie drove them the rest of the way home with as much speed as the law would allow. He decided that they should go to his house instead of his Grandmother's place where Derek lived because even though Maggie was gone Jamie still would feel funny about having sex in her home. When they got to the house, Jamie wanted to get Derek in a more undressed state. He took him in his arms and started unbuttoning his shirt. He took one button at a time stopping to kiss his lips lightly then started on the next button. Derek found this so erotic. He was on fire and wanted to hurry to the next phase, but Jamie had a whole different plan, taking everything real slow. All of a sudden he came to the realization that the slowing down and taking his good ole time was bringing a conversation front and center. "We take our time with everything that we do." *What are you doing Walker? Is this really what (or* whom *is a better word) you want?*

Like an omen, the phone rang. But before Jamie could get to it, the answer machine picked it up. He heard this deep, sexy voice which he recognized immediately.

"Mr. Walker, this is Mr. Morgan. I just wanted to let you know that I am driving Shadow to you in the next couple of days. Let me know if this is not convenient for you. You know the number. If I don't hear from you, I will assume that it's okay and I'll start out. It will take me about two days. Thanks for being so patient with this transaction. I know you're anxious to get your horse."

"That's not all I am anxious about," he thought. He stopped, "I'm sorry Derek, but I can't do this."

"What? Why have you changed your mind? Did I do something wrong? I thought you wanted me as much as I wanted you. You sure acted like it in the car."

"I did — but now I just can't do it."

"Oh, I see. You get a phone call and everything is stopped. Well that's fine, I don't want to be with someone who doesn't want me, too." Derek buttoned his shirt back up and excused himself. He had wanted Jamie for a very long time, but he was not going to prostitute himself if this is not a mutual situation. He realized that the voice on the phone was really what was bothering Jamie. "So, this whole thing with staying in Wyoming an extra day was about this sexy voice," Derek thought. "At least I had a taste — *literally!* — of what it would have been like to be with Jamie for a short while . . ."

———•••———

Marc hung up the phone and was disappointed that he didn't get to talk to Jamie instead of his voice on the answer machine. He had made the decision to bring Shadow to Jamie himself because he couldn't stand the thought of never seeing Jamie again. He had to see him again to see if there really was a strong chemistry that was like a magnet pulling them toward each other. It seemed beyond their control. *So, why did you send him packing you fool? He's what you want, and you knew it then! Why didn't you go into his room that night when you stood outside his door? You are your own worst enemy, Marc Morgan.*

———

Jamie tried to sleep that night, but sleep eluded him. All he could think about was that Marc would be here in another couple of days.

"God, Jamie, you have it bad."

CHEYENNE LOVE

CHAPTER FOUR

DRIVING TO BEREA, KENTUCKY

Marc decided he should probably bring Keith with him to handle Shadow until Jamie got used to him and that Shadow adjusted well to his new surroundings.

"Keith, I need you to go with me to Berea, Kentucky to help with Shadow, so if you would, get him ready to travel and pack a bag. We'll be there for about a week.

Marc paced the floor that night because he couldn't stop thinking about seeing Jamie again. He hadn't heard from Jamie, so he knew he was up for having him bring the horse. That was a good sign.

Jamie could not get it off his mind that Marc was leaving tomorrow for here. He wanted to see him so bad. He, too, was not able to sleep, but he hadn't slept much since the phone call.

Early next morning, Marc and Keith loaded Shadow into the horse trailer and started off to Kentucky. Marc had butterflies in his stomach thinking about seeing the beautiful blond that had taken over his every waking thought.

"Do you think with stops along the way we could

make it to Kentucky in one day? I did a MapQuest and it's 1259.67 miles to Berea, so it'll take us about 18 hours 51 minutes, without stops. If we start at 4am, we should be there around 11pm if you include all stops."

"Marc, what's the hurry? Shadow will need some breaks in the travel. We should stop and lead him out of the trailer and let him walk around a little. Do you have to get there sooner than what you originally said? It'd be better for the horse if we stopped over night — but if you need to get there sooner, then I guess we could do it."

"Well, I'd just like to get there sooner. The sooner we get there, the sooner we can get back. I have a lot of work here on the ranch that I can't leave unattended for very long — but then I don't have to tell you that."

"Are you sure that's the real reason for this fast track to Berea? It couldn't be about Mr. Walker, could it?" Keith had noticed the tension between them when Jamie was at the ranch. He suspected that they were dancing around each other trying to figure out what they both were feeling. Keith was gay and saw all the signs of Marc being gay, but until this Walker guy came Marc had not shown any attraction towards another man.

"Excuse me, I don't think that is any of your business. You just keep your mind where it should be, with Shadow. I will take care of Mr. Walker." *Boy that is the truth; I will take care of Mr. Walker,* Marc thought to himself.

"Okay, I sure didn't mean any disrespect." Keith stopped talking and just watched the road.

They drove for hours on end, only stopping long enough for gas, bathroom breaks, food and to exercise Shadow. Marc was driven — like a man on a mission, Keith noticed. Marc knew he was being ridiculous about traveling like this but he couldn't stop himself. He wanted to see Jamie that bad.

They arrived at Berea at 11pm. He told Keith to go ahead and walk the horse and he would give Jamie a call to tell him they were there and to get directions to the farm. Jamie answered on the first ring. God, Walker, you are really giving it away that you're anxious to hear from Marc. "Hello, this is the Walker homestead," Jamie spoke with more calm than he thought he would.

"Hello, Mr. Walker, this is Marc Morgan. I've arrived here in Berea. I know it's late, but I want to bring the horse to your ranch tonight so that he can move around. He's been in the trailer for most of the day. Can you give me the instructions on how to get there?"

"Just come on down the main drag through town and when you start seeing country, turn at the first road. You can only turn one way. Come on down the road until you see the first house — that's the farmhouse; the stables are in that barn right behind the house. My house is a little farther down the road. We'll be waiting at the farmhouse for you."

Jamie was so nervous inside he could hardly contain himself. "How will Marc act when he sees me again?," Jamie wondered. He called down to the barn and told Derek that they were in town and on their way to the farm. He checked in the mirror to see how he looked and then headed over to the barn. When he walked in, Derek did a double take. Jamie was wearing a beautiful brown sweater that brought out the brown and gold flecks in his eyes and skin tight jeans that didn't leave much to the imagination. Derek thought he looked good enough to eat. All of a sudden he resented this Marc guy because he was going to get what he wanted and almost had. Things had been a little strained between him and Jamie but they were working past it. He knew that Marc was what Jamie wanted — that was very obvious when he heard the deep sexy voice on the phone.

Marc and Keith were driving up to the barn when Derek came out of the barn to help with Shadow. Keith noticed how great he looked right away. "Wow, I'm going to enjoy this week I think." Marc asked him what he said. Keith just looked at him. "...Nothing."

Marc climbed out of the truck and started helping with Shadow. Jamie walked out of the barn. Marc almost dropped the gate to the trailer. Jamie looked so amazing that he took Marc's breath away. *How can any one man look that good and still be real?* Jamie walked up to Marc and put out his hand.

"Welcome to the Walker farm." Marc took Jamie's hand and shook it but then didn't let it go. They both stood there looking at each other. Marc looked at Jamie's lips. "I want to kiss you so much", Marc thought. Jamie could pretty much read Marc's mind. "Me too," Jamie said out loud. Marc shook his head a little and let go of Jamie.

Jamie grinned because he knew that Marc wasn't expecting that comment.

Marc turned to Keith trying to shake off the excitement he felt with Jamie's comment. "Keith, let's get Shadow unloaded." Derek walked around to the back of the trailer to help. Jamie introduced him to Marc and then Marc introduced Derek to Keith. They shook hands and then went into the barn together to get Shadow settled. They put him into the stall which Jamie had made for him. Derek noticed Keith looking at him, and realized by the way he was checking him out that he was gay. "This could be fun," Derek thought.

"Let's go into the house and get something to eat. Are you two hungry?" Jamie asked.

"Yeah, we could use some food, and maybe a beer if you have one." Marc responded with more control than he thought he would have.

"Derek, come on in to eat with us when you get Shadow settled."

"I'll help you, Derek," Keith said a little too eager. "That's okay, Keith. I can handle it." Keith looked disappointed but decided to let it drop. The other three went into the house and Jamie started getting some stuff out for sandwiches. Meanwhile Derek finished up and came in just as they sat down to eat. He noticed the empty seat left for him was next to Keith. *Cool. That works for me. He is really cute — a little eager, but cute.*

Marc and Jamie were sitting, talking about the horse, the drive here and any other small talk they could think of. Both were very antsy about being together again. Jamie could feel Marc's knee against his and also noticed that he didn't try to move it. The spot felt like it was burning. Jamie wanted to touch his knee with his hand and move his hand on up his inner thigh. Marc must have been reading Jamie's mind because he laid his right hand on Jamie's knee. Jamie made a small groan sound, which encouraged Marc to go further. He started moving his hand up Jamie's inner thigh. He was getting really close to Jamie's groin and Jamie wondered if he was going to stop there. "Oh my god," he thought. "What is he trying to do to me? Can't he see I want him and need him?"

Marc did know what he was doing to Jamie and he felt the same. He was not going to push Jamie away from him this time. He was determined to have what he craved. He had to think of some way to get him alone. Jamie opened the door himself.

Trying to get his voice to stay steady, Jamie said "Marc, I'd like to walk you out to the pond and show you how beautiful it is at this time of night. I also would like to show you where I live."

"You don't live here?"

"No, this was my grandmother's farmhouse and I didn't want to live in it. I wanted a place of my own. Derek lives here. Keith automatically looked up. *Oh boy, this is really going to be fun.* Derek and Keith's eyes met with this revelation.

"About the walk — I think Keith and I should get settled into a hotel before we do anything else." Marc said it, but hoped they wouldn't have to leave. Keith was disappointed that Marc even suggested it. He wanted to stay here at the farm and see what could come up between him and Derek. He grinned when he thought of what might come up between them.

"Of course you are not going to stay in a hotel. We have plenty of bedrooms here at the farm; my grandmother's house alone has five bedrooms and mine has seven. I think we can put you up here."

"Hey Derek, why don't you take Keith upstairs and show him to one of the guest rooms. You should probably stay here with Derek, Keith, because you guys will be working with the horse. If you don't mind, Marc, I would like you to stay with me at the main house because we'll have to talk business regarding the horse, etc. Are these arrangement suitable with both of you?"

"Sure, that's very nice of you. It'll be easier to take care of business this way. Maybe by staying here, we can get things done sooner and Keith and I can get back to Wyoming sooner." Marc knew this was not what was going to happen, but this is what he wanted Jamie to think.

Derek took Keith upstairs and showed him where he could stay. As they entered the room, Keith asked Derek if he was gay. Derek looked him in the eye, "You know I am. You know I saw you checking me out and I was not offended, so what do you want to do about this turn of events? It looks like we're going to be left on our own."

"Well, I would like to get to know you better. Maybe we can start with another beer and talk a little."

"That works for me. Let's go back down to the kitch-en. We'll talk and get more comfortable with each other." Derek was getting a new chance. He knew Jamie was into Marc — the tension was so thick you could cut it with a knife. So why shouldn't he see what might develop with Keith? *He is really good looking and I am really horny.*

———————

Jamie and Marc started walking to the pond. Marc would drive the truck over to Jamie's house later. He re-ally wanted to be alone with Jamie. Jamie was feeling the same way and for some reason he was really nervous. "Is he going to kiss me again?" Jamie wondered. His palms were sweaty and his groin was crying. He had never been attracted to anyone like this man. He wanted to be with him so bad, and he would never just jump into bed with someone so easy, but he would do whatever this cowboy wanted and not worry about the consequences.

They continued the walk to the pond in silence. When they got there, Jamie stopped and told Marc this is his fa-vorite place in the world. Marc was watching Jamie's face in the moonlight and had never seen anyone more beau-tiful. His blond hair was shinning in the moon's glow. "God, I want to do this right but I am not sure I can keep myself under control being around him," Marc thought.

"Marc? Why are you not talking?"

Marc couldn't stand it any longer. He moved very swiftly and took Jamie in his arms. He kissed his most kissable lips, with all the passion that he had been think-ing about doing ever since he sent him away. He groaned out loud when Jamie responded by opening his mouth for Marc's tongue to enter. Marc licked him everywhere inside his warm mouth. Their tongues were dancing together and one was no more demanding than the other. Their breathing became erratic and both men were so consumed with the other. The outside world no longer existed. Finally, they came up for air. Neither one knew who broke the kiss, but when they separated their lips they stood in silence staring at each other.

"Jamie, I have no idea what's happened to me since I met you — but you have taken over my entire life. I can't think of anything else but you. I had to bring the horse so that I could do this." He took possession of Jamie's lips again and Jamie was melting into a heap of mush, making small, faint sounds that were making Marc crazy. Against Jamie's lips Marc whispered, "I want you so much and this is so hard for me because I have never felt this way for any other man. I can't get you out of my mind." He broke the kiss again and kept Jamie held firmly in his arms but moved his head back so that he could see Jamie's eyes.

"Do you feel for me anything even remotely close to what I feel for you?" Marc asked.

"Yes, Marc. I haven't thought of anyone but you since you sent me away. Why did you do that? You could have had me then if you would have just entered my room that night when you were outside the door. I would not have been able to deny you anything."

"Okay, I'm knocking at your bedroom door. Will you

let me in now?" Marc asked. Jamie answered him by once more kissing him and then taking his very handsome cowboy by the hand and leading him to his house with the promise of heaven on earth.

CHAPTER FIVE

HEAVEN ON EARTH

Jamie led Marc around to the house. When they got inside, Marc pulled Jamie back into an embrace. "Jamie, I want you to know something before we go any further."

"What? What is it?" Jamie asked, a little worried. Was he going tell him that this was going to be a one-time thing and when he goes back to Cheyenne, this will be done?

Marc saw the look of concern on Jamie's face and quickly spoke. "I have never been with a man before because I didn't want to unless it was for a real relationship. I can't just sleep with you and then be pushed aside. I don't want meaningless sex. That is not me. If we do this, you will be mine and I will be yours and only yours."

Jamie was so moved by Marc's words and relieved that Marc wasn't going to leave him after. Jamie put both hands on Marc's cheeks and pulled him down into a very sweet but emotional kiss as tears formed in Marc's eyes. At that moment, he knew he loved this wonderful, handsome cowboy and he was going to show him how much.

"Marc, come knock on my bedroom door like you asked me if you could. I want to let you into my bedroom, my heart and my life."

Jamie led him to the master bedroom. The room was huge and the bed was a big four-poster king. Marc stopped outside and smiled at Jamie. "You go in and shut the door. I'll give you a minute or so, and then I'm going to knock." He knew this was so silly but he wanted to do it anyway. Jamie did as he asked, and when he shut the door he raced to get his clothes off. He wanted to be standing, waiting, when Marc knocked. He lit some candles and dimmed the lights in the room. He was ready.

Marc figured he had waited long enough, so he tapped on the door. Both of them knew this was so laughable, but it was sort of symbolic too. Jamie told Marc to come in. Marc opened the door and stopped dead still. The picture before him was unbelievable. Jamie was standing in the candle-lit room with nothing on. Marc didn't think he could move; the site mesmerized him. Jamie's skin and hair were glowing in this light. He was absolutely the most exquisite thing he had ever laid eyes on. He looked like a Greek god ,only with blonde hair. Marc took a couple of steps farther into the room. He never took his eyes off Jamie.

"I have never seen anything in my life that I wanted more than you right this moment."

"Come here, Marc, come close to me." Jamie motioned. Marc closed the distance between them in two steps. He touched Jamie's face and then moved his hands down Jamie's magnificent body. Jamie started unbuttoning Marc's shirt and pulled it off, pants next. When he slipped Marc's jeans and briefs down and off, he exposed

Marc's manhood. Jamie uttered a sound that Marc had never heard before. Jamie had to touch Marc. He brushed his hand against Marc's hip and groin, causing Marc to grab Jamie and pull him against him.

"God Jamie, your touch sets me on fire. I have never felt this before. Please show me how to make you happy."

Jamie knelt down in front of Marc and took him into his hands. He kissed the head and all the way down the shaft with tiny kisses. He handled Marc's balls with such gentle care and licked them. Marc started moaning and his breath was coming faster. "Oh my god!" he cried. Jamie then took him in his mouth and gently, with his teeth, moved very slowly up the shaft to the tip. This was driving Marc insane. Jamie licked up the back of his cock and then took him back into his mouth. Marc thought there could be no better feeling in the world than this sensation that Jamie was causing with his mouth. Jamie started moving up and down now with a smooth rhythmic motion that sent Marc over the top. He came in Jamie's mouth pulsating with so many waves, and Jamie took it all. He licked Marc clean and stood up to face him. Marc kissed him and ran his tongue into Jamie's warm wet mouth; the mouth that had given him so much pleasure. Jamie was starting to ache from his own need to come. Marc noticed and took Jamie over to the bed. They climbed in and Marc laid Jamie on his back. Marc moved on down to give Jamie the same pleasure he had just given him. He moved up and down Jamie with his mouth wrapped around Jamie's dick. He was not practiced at this, so he stumbled a little but caught on pretty quick, when he heard the sounds of pleasure coming out of Jamie. As aroused as Jamie was it didn't take long before Jamie started coming. Marc was unsure about swallowing Jamie's cum but when he tasted it he wanted it all.

They stayed wrapped in each other's arms and just were. Neither wanted to leave the other.

"Jamie, are you happy right now?"

"Yes Marc, I couldn't be happier. Why do you ask? Don't you think we were good together?"

"Of course! I think we were great, but since I'm not experienced I had my concerns." Jamie was so amazed that a personality as strong as Marc, a man who owns a huge 750-acre ranch, could be so vulnerable and unsure when it comes to making love. But Jamie was willing to teach him. Jamie wrapped his arms around Marc really tight and snuggled against him. "You are good enough for me. I want to sleep in your arms and wake up in them in the morning. Just hold me and don't let me go." They slept. Tomorrow was another day.

Chapter Six

Coming Together

Derek and Keith talked most of the night. They felt the need to get to know each other. They would be working together, at least until the horse was settled in.

"Keith, how do you like the farm — what little you've seen of it?"

"I like it fine, but what I like most about it is meeting you. What are your duties here?"

"We can talk about that tomorrow. How long have you been with Mr. Morgan? Have you two ever......?"

Keith cut him off. "No — Heavens, no. He's been waiting for just the right man to come along, and it looks to me that he's found him. It was quite obvious the way he reacted in Cheyenne when your boss came to visit us. Also, what gave it away was when he said he was going to bring the horse himself. I knew then that this guy was special. The final thing was that we had to drive non-stop to get here."

"Well, I'm glad that you came with him."

"Me too."

"Well, we'd better get some sleep. I have a feeling we're going to have an early day tomorrow. Do you remember where your bedroom was?"

"Yes — but aren't you going to escort me up there?" Keith asked with a smile on his face.

"I think you're a big boy and can find your own way. I have to shut everything down and lock up. You'll be fine alone." He grinned at the hurt look on Keith's face. He knew he was feeling playful.

Keith went up and Derek started locking up and turning lights off. As he was walking up the stairs to his bedroom he ran straight into Keith. "What do you think you're doing? You scared me to death. I wasn't expecting to run into you in the hall."

Keith moved closer and put his hands on Derek's cheeks. "I have wanted to do this every since you walked out of the barn this evening." He kissed Derek very softly. Derek responded very quickly. He opened his mouth to let Keith in and kissed him deeply, matching kiss for kiss, lick for lick. "I want to spend the night with you, Derek. I want to show you how much being with me would do for you."

Derek pushed him away. "What? What do you think, that you're that hot? That no one can resist you? With an ego like that, you can forget about getting me into bed with you. I don't need you to show me how to...Oh hell, get out of my way." Derek pushed on past Keith and headed to his bedroom. When he got there he made sure the door was locked. "How dare he," Derek thought. "He is good looking, but not *that* damn good looking."

"God, what an ego." Derek got undressed and went to bed. About 4am he was awakened by a knock on his door.

He knew it was Keith. He got up and went to the door.

"What do you want?"

"I want to come in and talk to you. I don't want us to get off on the wrong foot and I couldn't sleep until I apologized to you for what I said to you. Please Derek, open the door and let me in."

"Keith, it's 4am in the morning. We can talk tomorrow." Derek went back to bed.

Keith knocked again. "Please, Derek, let me in. I promise I won't attack you."

Derek knew that he was not going to get any more sleep if he didn't let him say what he wanted. He went over to the door and unlocked it. Keith heard the lock move and he opened the door. He stood there unsure how to do this. Derek lost his patience. "Okay, Keith, what do you want to say? Let's get this over with so I can get some sleep. I have a lot of chores to do in the morning."

"I'll help you with them. Just listen to me. I am sorry for being so crude. I didn't mean to come off like some Casanova. I'm not that experienced with men...but I wanted you so bad and just didn't handle it well."

"Apology accepted. Now, can I get some sleep? Go away." Derek turned to go back to the bed when Keith grabbed his arm, pulling him close.

"I want you," he said, as he moved his hand down to Derek's cock. He touched him and got a response almost immediately. Derek only had pajama bottoms on and nothing else. He groaned a little when Keith touched him and wanted him to continue. Keith knew that his hand was not rejected and he kept getting braver. He reached in the front of Derek's pajamas and took him into his hand. He moved up and down a couple of times until Derek was leaking some pre-cum. "Derek, I want to continue but not unless you say you want me to. Do you want me to keep on?"

"Yes," he whispered, "I want you to keep on." Derek was really feeling good under Keith's expert hands. Keith took both hands and worked Derek up and down. Derek was moving his hips forward, wanting more. Keith pulled Derek's pants off and Derek was standing completely naked. He pulled Keith over to the bed and laid down, pulling Keith on top of him. Keith started stripping his pajama bottoms off, too, and both men laid naked with their bodies touching in every way. Keith moved down and took Derek in his mouth. He held his balls and stroked up and down on Derek and gently massaged his balls at the same time. He licked up the back of his dick and then down to the sensitive spot between his dick and his balls. He licked around the balls and down further between his rectum and the base of his balls. Derek was moaning for Keith to move faster. Keith took him back in his mouth and moved rapidly until Derek came. They both came down from the throws of passion and just stayed very still in each other's arms.

"I can't believe I let you do that. I had no intention of having anymore to do with you. God, can you persuade a guy to change his mind."

"I wanted you and I know, regardless of what you said,

you wanted me too — until I opened my big mouth and inserted my foot."

"That is a colorful description, but I can think of something else that's much better inserted in your big mouth than your foot." Both men laughed and hugged.

"You owe me, Derek." Keith smiled as he told him that, and Derek shook his head.

"Let's get some sleep, okay?" They both closed their eyes and drifted off.

———

Marc woke up first and still had Jamie lying in his arms. He smiled, and remembered last night. God, Jamie was so easy on the eyes and so wonderful to be with. He was so glad he had waited for Jamie to come into his life. He pulled him closer and kissed him on the forehead. Jamie started stirring and looked up at Marc with sleep in his eyes. Marc whispered in Jamie's ear, "I am falling in love with you."

Jamie heard that and sat up, wiping the sleep from his eyes. "Did you say what I think you said?"

"Yes Jamie, I am falling in love with you."

"I think I'm falling in love with you, too, but how can this be? We just met. We don't even know anything about each other. I do know, though, that I can't get you off my mind. You have occupied every waking hour of my days since I met you. I just want to be with you." Jamie said this as he went back into Marc's arms.

Marc hugged him with all the strength that he had and told Jamie that he just wants to be with him also. Marc claimed Jamie's lips, his mouth and his tongue. Their kiss was getting deeper and more urgent. When they stopped kissing, Jamie was trying to get his breath under control. "Do you know how you make my heart, my body and my mind want you *totally,* Marc? I want to crawl into your skin. It's as though I can't get close enough to you. God, you have totally possessed my soul."

Marc's breath caught, listening to Jamie describe his feelings for him. All he could say was that he feels the same way. Jamie wanted to instantly lighten the mood. He thought they needed to talk about the heavy stuff later on tonight, maybe, over dinner, wine and candlelight. Right now he wanted to go ride with Marc and show him his grounds. "Marc, let's get up and shower and take a ride before breakfast. What do you say? I want to show you my home."

"Okay," Marc said very reluctantly. "I guess I can wait 'til tonight to have you all to myself. I want to really make love to you, Jamie." Jamie knew what he was trying to say, and he knew that even though he had never given himself completely to another man, he was ready to do so with Marc. He also knew that Marc had never been with a man before so they were going to have to learn how together.

"Let's get up, Marc," Jamie said as he pulled him out of bed and headed him to the shower. I'll go in the one off the other bedroom down the hall."

"Ahh, Jamie, why don't you shower with me? It would be so much more fun."

"I know — that's the *exact* reason why I am not going there with you. We would never get out of this bedroom!"

Marc was feeling playful. "So? What's wrong with that?" He grinned.

"Get in there," as he pushed him toward the bathroom. "I'm outta here." Jamie waited until Marc headed to the bathroom, when he all of a sudden ran over to Marc and grabbed him, spun him around, and kissed him quickly on the mouth and then ran out before Marc could react. He heard Marc holler at him as he left the room, "You're in trouble now, Walker!"

CHEYENNE LOVE

CHAPTER SEVEN

WALKER'S POND

Jamie and Marc finished getting ready for their ride. Jamie got downstairs first and waited anxiously for Marc to come down. When he spotted him on the stairs he almost fainted. Marc was wearing black jeans, black western shirt, black cowboy boots and a black cowboy hat. With his flowing, black hair and blue eyes, he was the most stunning looking man Jamie had ever seen. "Wow, this gorgeous man is going to be totally mine soon." Jamie thought. "Thank you, Lord, for sending me to Cheyenne to buy a horse!"

Marc noticed the expression on Jamie's face. "You like what you see, Jamie?" he asked as he came down and walked right up to Jamie.

"Oh, I don't know, I guess you'll do." He closed the small distance between them and put his lips on Marc's wonderful mouth. Marc reacted by pulling Jamie into his arms and opened Jamie's mouth with his insistent tongue. Jamie started moaning wanting more. Marc finally released Jamie's luscious lips and stood smiling at him.

"Now, will I *just* do?"

Jamie was still trying to get his breath back. "Yep, you will *more* than do. I think I'll keep you around."

"You bet your sweet ass you will!" Marc laughed as he went past Jamie to head to the barn to get their horses ready for their ride. Jamie had already called Derek to get two horses saddled for their ride. When they got down there, they noticed that Derek and Keith were pretty friendly. They were standing very close and had shit-eatin' grins on their faces.

"What have you two been up to?" Marc asked. "You both look like you've been up all night. Hmm...let me see...been in bed with each other all night?"

"Maybe," Keith said and smiled at Derek. Derek walked past Keith and smacked him on the butt.

Jamie and Marc got on the horses and set off on their morning ride around the property. Jamie was really anxious to show Marc what he owned and how beautiful it is here. They road hard, and even challenged each other to a race. Having their horses in full gallops across the fields, Marc noticed how beautiful Jamie was on the horse with the wind blowing his blond tresses back off his face. He looked as if he was one with the horse. Jamie was watching Marc also. He sat in the saddle like a man who really knew what he was doing. It was obvious that he rides all the time and was very comfortable in the saddle. They finally pulled the horses to a stop and got off to walk around the pond. They walked for a while, leading their horses and then finally tying them to a tree.

"Let's go sit by the pond," Jamie suggested. Marc moved beside him and sat down. He did think this was a very pretty place and so peaceful. The water in the pond was so clear that you could almost see the bottom, and the area was surrounded by trees — huge, beautiful oaks which had obviously been around for several hundred years. *This place must be steeped in history,* Marc observed. *Probably dating back to early 1800s.* He could see why Jamie thought this place was so special.

"Jamie, come sit closer to me," as he patted the spot next to him. Jamie did as he was asked.

Marc put his arm around Jamie's shoulder and pulled him down on the ground laying him flat. He moved onto Jamie and pinned him under his body. He started at his lips and kissed him lightly and then moved to his ear and neck. Jamie was starting to feel himself melting under Marc's lips. Marc kept his assault going down Jamie's neck and on down to the area on his neck that was exposed by the open collar. As he did so, he started unbuttoning Jamie's shirt. When he got all the buttons undone he opened the shirt to expose the beautiful chest and abs of Jamie.

"God, Jamie, you are so beautiful." He put his hands on Jamie's chest and gently touched his nipple with his fingers. Jamie moaned. Hearing that sound come out of Jamie, Marc kissed his nipple and licked around it, flicking it with his tongue. This was driving Jamie crazy. Jamie whispered Marc's name and begged, "...please!" Marc was so turned on by this that he moved his hands across his chest and fondled him all the way down to his belt buckle. Jamie was breathing heavy and moving under Marc. He whispered Marc's name again, and Marc just about came in his jeans at the sound of his name softly on Jamie's lips. He has never felt like this before and he didn't want this feeling to end. As he kissed Jamie again on his soft lips, he put his hand on Jamie's crotch. Jamie let out a moan and moved his hips forward, pushing his hard cock in Marc's hand.

"Marc...Marc..." Jamie was muttering and moving his head from side to side. "Please, take me in your mouth. You are driving me crazy!" That was all Marc needed to hear. He immediately pulled Jamie's jeans and briefs off. He went down on Jamie and took him into his mouth. He started moving up and down while sucking at the same time. Jamie was almost screaming in ecstasy. Jamie kept thinking: *I want to stop this because I want Marc in my mouth also.* He suddenly pulled Marc's head up and told him to please take his pants off.

"I want to take you in my mouth. I want to do this together."

"What do you mean, Jamie?...I don't understand..."

"Just take your Jeans off and I'll show you." Marc did as he asked. "Now, lay down. I promise you won't regret it." Marc lay on the ground and Jamie took his position over Marc with his head at Marc's feet. Marc looked up and had Jamie's dick in his face. Jamie took Marc in his mouth and started moving up and down. Marc was getting the idea now and took Jamie back in his mouth. They worked together until they both came. They were in heaven with each one tasting the other. It was so powerful. Marc had learned something new again with Jamie.

"That was amazing, Jamie. I love being with you. It's like I can't get enough of you! Let's get out of the rest of our clothes and have a swim before we go back to the house for breakfast. The water looks so inviting."

"Okay, Marc, whatever you want. Last one in is a rotten egg!" Jamie started running to the pond with Marc on his heels. They swam and played and kissed. They were so into each other and their desires to claim the other one. When they had almost worn themselves out they climbed out of the water and got dressed again. As they mounted their horses, Jamie looked at Marc, "I want to be yours forever." Marc shook his head as if to say, "Me too."

Cheyenne Love

Chapter Eight

Dinner for Two

They rode back to the barn and turned the horses over to Derek to brush down. Keith was out in the exercise ring riding Shadow around. Jamie came up to Derek and asked him about last night.

"Are you and Keith getting along okay? It looks to me and Marc that you did more than chat last night."

"Yes, you could say that. We did have a good time. You'll have to thank Marc for me. I'm so glad he brought Keith with him. Speaking of Marc, how are you two getting along? I could tell he was important to you when he called and you heard his voice. I knew then that I didn't have a chance with you. I really care about you, Jamie, and I want you to be happy. I knew when I saw that constant grin on your face since he got here that you are. I just hope he doesn't hurt you! What's going to happen with the two of you when he goes back to Cheyenne?"

"He'll move here, I'm sure. Maybe Keith will come here to live with Marc. You'd like that, wouldn't you?"

"I wouldn't be too sure about that! I don't think he's going to give up his ranch."

"Yes, he will; he loves me." About that time Marc came into the stable.

"Who loves you?" he said as he came up behind Jamie.

"Why, who do you think?" They both laughed and headed to the house. Derek was not laughing though, because he felt Jamie was in for some heartbreak.

Keith brought Shadow into the stall and brushed him down, put some oats in the feeder and came out to stand with Derek. "Keith, do you think Marc will ever leave Cheyenne and move here with Jamie?"

"Heavens, no. Jamie will have to move to Wyoming if he wants to be with Marc. Why do you ask, did he say he would?"

"No, Jamie just thinks that Marc will be willing to stay here."

"Never happen, I assure you."

———————

The day went by very quickly and Jamie was getting so anxious to have dinner with Marc. He had a lot of things planned for tonight and he wanted everything to be just so. Jamie gave all the instructions to the cook and butler and went up to take a shower and get ready. Marc had already gone up to his room. When he heard Jamie come up the stairs, he stuck his head out of the door and grabbed Jamie as he passed.

"Marc, what are you doing?" as he was being dragged into his room. Marc didn't answer but pulled Jamie close, put both hands on his cheeks and claimed Jamie's lips.

"God, I love kissing you. I can never get enough!"

"I enjoy it, too, but you're going to have to let me go and get ready for our dinner."

"Okay, okay, I'll let you go for now — but tonight I'm not going to let you slip away. You're gonna be mine! I want to possess you, body and soul!"

"You'll get your chance later, I promise."

They had spent the entire day together talking, and working with Derek, Keith and Shadow. Jamie told Marc of his plans for Shadow. He shared with Marc the best-selling books he had written — none of which Marc had read, he confessed, as they just weren't his "cup of tea." They were fictional stories of historical time travel, with the main character falling in love with someone from another time. Marc said he preferred reading non-fiction, such as books about Indians and their interactions with white settlers. Jamie told Marc that his next book would take place in Cheyenne, Wyoming with a very handsome Indian warrior, written just for him. They laughed about that. "You write it, and I'll read it!"

Marc came down to dinner first. He had struggled with what to wear, but finally decided on starched jeans, cowboy boots and a red western shirt that looked incredibly good on him with his black hair and blue eyes. Maurice (Jamie's butler) asked Marc what he would like to drink. Marc settled on a beer and waited in the lounge for Jamie to come down.

Jamie came into the lounge, and when Marc turned around his heart skipped a beat and he gasped out loud. "Thank you, Lord, for giving him to me," he thought. Jamie wore a pair of jeans, gold button-down shirt that was the same color as his hair and showing off his golden brown eyes. Jamie was so pleased that his looks got that kind of response from Marc. Marc immediately closed the distance across the room and took Jamie into his arms kissing him passionately, sliding his tongue into Jamie's warm mouth and smothering him with kisses all over his face and neck.

"You know that you are knock-down gorgeous and I want to do all kinds of great-but-naughty things to you. I'm not sure I can wait 'til after dinner to take you completely and make you a part of me."

Jamie teasingly said, "Well, I guess you will have to wait because we are going to eat first."

"Oh, okay, but then . . ."

They walked hand-in-hand into the dinning room. Lights were out and the candles were lit all around the room. The table was set and ready for them to have a very intimate dinner. Wine was poured, soft music played in the background and the first course was being served. Marc kept staring at Jamie because he was absolutely the most beautiful thing he had ever seen with the candlelight dancing in his eyes! Marc couldn't help himself,. He leaned over the table and briefly kissed Jamie and whispered, "I'm lost every time I look at you. I can't think straight, so you'll have to lead me through this night!"

Jamie was so taken with Marc's words that tears formed in his eyes. "I know this is really soon since we've only known each other a couple of weeks, but I want you to know that I do love you, Marc."

Marc was so happy to hear that he was not the only one feeling the draw between them. He had never encountered anyone like Jamie and as soon as he saw him he knew he was hooked. "Jamie, I am in love with you too. Let's finish dinner so we can go on with our wonderful, exciting evening. That is, if you want to finish dinner."

Jamie got up walked around the table and pulled Marc up by the hand. "You want me to lead you through the night, well let's go on that journey."

Jamie led and Marc followed. He took Marc up to his bedroom suite and opened the door. When he did, Marc couldn't believe his eyes. There were candles everywhere in the room and all lit. It looked like hundreds, but Marc knew that it couldn't be that many. There was a fire in the fireplace and a beautiful, thick, plush, white bearskin rug on the floor in front of the fire. He had very soft music playing and the whole room smelled of jasmine. Jamie had planned it to be perfect for their first time together.

He pulled Marc into the room and shut the door behind them. "Marc, I want to take this slow and savor every moment of our lovemaking." He pulled Marc over in front of the fireplace and moved in close so he could start undoing his shirt. "God, Marc, you look so good in red. Well for that matter you look good in anything you put on, but now I want you without any clothes." He pushed the shirt off Marc's shoulders and as he did he moved his hands down his arms until the shirt hit the floor. He then put his hands on Marc's chest and felt his pecs, moving his hands very softly across his chest. Marc was in heaven. He loved feeling Jamie's hands on him. When Jamie licked his nipple and gently sucked on it, Marc thought he had never felt anything so erotic and wonderful. He started responding by trying to kiss Jamie's neck. Jamie let him kiss his neck for a short time, but he wanted to be in control for a while. He put his hands on Marc's belt buckle and started to undo it. Marc sighed and closed his eyes. Jamie ran his hand down the front of Marc's jeans and found his target. Marc made a small sound and opened his eyes. He looked straight into Jamie's golden brown eyes and saw the lust and love that was shining back at him. Marc's dick was so hard, but he agreed with Jamie — he wanted this to last. He started undoing Jamie's shirt, one button at a time. He ran his hands under Jamie's shirt and around to his back, pulling him up against his bare skin. The sensation of Jamie's skin touching his was very addicting. They held each other bare chest to bare chest, wrapped together. Jamie kissed Marc's lips very slow, licking his lips and putting his tongue on his lower lip so that Marc would let him in. Marc's mouth opened and Jamie moved in. He kept kissing him and licking all around his wonderful mouth. He could feel Marc's hard dick against his and it was driving him crazy.

They pulled away and just stared at each other for a second and then started rubbing chest-to-chest, mouth-to-mouth, tongues dancing together in perfect unison. Marc started undoing Jamie's jeans, pushing them down, then his own. He stepped out of his jeans and Jamie followed suit. Neither one had worn underwear anticipating this very thing. They didn't want anything between them. Marc wanted to feel Jamie all over. They rubbed their groins together feeling the want between them. Jamie moved away from Marc and laid down on the rug in front of the fire. He reached up for Marc to join him. When he looked down at Jamie, he had never wanted anything this much before. He knelt down and kissed Jamie again. "Jamie, I want you so bad. I hope I can last long enough!"

"It will be wonderful Marc, you'll see." Jamie encouraged Marc to lie down beside him. They wrapped their arms around each other and pressed their bodies close enough to know that each one could come anytime. Marc leaned up and positioned himself to be able to taste Jamie's cock. He ran his tongue down Jamie's cock and up around the head. He put his tongue in the slit at the top and heard the most wonderful sound come out of Jamie. Jamie was breathing heavy with his chest moving up and down faster and faster. Marc could taste the pre-cum and it was wonderful. He put his mouth over the head and took him entirely in his mouth. Moving up and down he ran his hand down around Jamie's balls and when he took hold of them Jamie cried out in ecstasy. He was moving his hips up and down.

"Marc...Marc...stop or I'm going to come."

"Yes, you are." Marc moved up and down again and Jamie filled his mouth with cum. It tasted so good and Marc licked him completely until Jamie came down from his orgasm.

"Marc, I want you deep inside of me. I have never given myself to another man and I want you to be my first and last. I have saved myself for you, the man I love."

"Jamie I'm not sure what to do since I've never done this."

"Marc, do what you feel is the right way."

Jamie shifted himself and spread his legs. Marc watched him and got the idea. Marc rubbed his hand over Jamie's cock to his butt. He loved the feel of Jamie in his hands. He moved farther back and touched Jamie's love spot. He paused and looked at Jamie.

"Jamie, are you sure you want to do this? We can stop if you want — I don't want you to feel you have to." Marc's real fear was that he was afraid he would hurt Jamie but also that he would disappoint him. He was so nervous that he was visibly shaking.

"Marc — I want this, please. Don't worry. You love me right?"

"You know I do. I came all the way from Cheyenne just so that I could be near you again. I have never done that for anyone else. If I was ever unsure about it before, it went away when I arrived and saw you again."

"You are not going to hurt me and I know you are not going to disappoint me. I've got some things that I'm told that we need. They're in that drawer over there."

Marc got up and went to get what they needed. Jamie had gotten a tube of lube and condoms. He came back to the rug and lay down again with Jamie. He was still hard so there wasn't much need for more foreplay. Jamie spread himself again and told Marc what he should do with the lube. Marc put some on his fingers and started toward his goal. First one finger and Jamie started to move around. Marc could feel how tight he was and worried again about hurting him. Jamie was becoming breathless with Marc moving his finger in and out of Jamie. He added another finger, and then he started spreading his fingers inside Jamie and going around in circles and in and out. By this time Jamie was really squirming underneath Marc. Marc watched his facial expressions and was getting so turned on just watching Jamie. He knew he was making him happy.

"Marc...please...I want you inside me."

Marc was so ready himself that he reached for the condom. He placed himself at the entrance to Jamie. Jamie raised his hips and stuffed one of the fireplace hearth pillows under him. He put his legs up around Marc's waist and opened his legs wider. Marc instinctively knew what to do from here. Both guys were so turned on and had raging hard-ons. He pushed forward and saw Jamie wince.

"Please Marc — make me yours," Jamie moaned. Just hearing him say his name while he was moaning was such a turn on. He moved in a little farther and was so amazed at how tight and hot Jamie felt around his dick. *God, he is everything.* He started moving back and forth and the more he moved the more Jamie moaned his name. Finally, Jamie couldn't take it anymore and he put his hands on the hearth above his head and pushed toward Marc as hard as he could, shoving Marc all the way into him. Marc let out a cry and grabbed Jamie's hips and pounded into him at a rapid pace. Jamie was working himself again and Marc kept coming into him hard.

"Jamie, Jamie, my love, you're mine and I'm yours and I am coommmmming! Oh, god!"

"I'm coming!" Jamie had also come about the same time. They were both so loud that it was hard to know what was going on. Waves of pleasure, until he was spent and laid down on Jamie's chest, laying his head in Jamie's cum. He licked some of it and ran his fingers in it and put them in Jamie's mouth. "Oh — *so* good."

They lay there for a few minutes, and then Marc was soft and slipped out of Jamie. Jamie hated him leaving his body. He had never felt anything like this before. He had given his virginity to Marc and now he belonged to him. Marc was coming down off cloud nine. He wrapped his arms around Jamie and just held him. Jamie was putting little kisses on Marc's face and nose.

"Jamie, I love you with all my heart. Please stay with me for always. Promise me."

"I promise my wonderful, handsome cowboy. I am yours and I will always be with you."

They cuddled for a long while and watched the logs crackling in the fireplace. After a while, the embers were getting lower.

"Do you want to get up and shower and go back down to finish our meal?" Jamie asked.

"No, I want to shower and then put some more logs on

the fire and lay on this rug and maybe have another taste of you. That's all the eating I need to do right now.

"Well, I led you through tonight; you can lead me through our life together."

CHEYENNE LOVE

CHAPTER NINE

THE SEPARATION

They spent every day together working with the horse during the day and making love every evening. They could not get enough of each other. It was the end of the week and Marc and Keith had to start getting ready to go home. That night Jamie and Marc knew they were going to have to make some decisions about where they go from here. Neither wanted to be separated from the other. At dinner that night, they started talking about the future.

"Marc, how long will it take you to settle the sale of your ranch in Cheyenne and move the horses and all here?"

Marc looked at Jamie in disbelief. "What are you talking about? I'm not selling my ranch; I thought you would move to Cheyenne with me. You can write your novels anywhere and I certainly have more room for both stables of horses at my ranch than you do here."

Jamie was shocked, he never thought about leaving his homestead. "Excuse me, Marc, but why do you think I can give up the only home I have ever known and just pick up and move to Cheyenne?"

Both men were starting to raise their voices a little. Maurice came in to see if all was okay. "Sir, can I get you and Mr. Morgan anything else to drink or eat?" He came in because he thought his presence would calm things down a little.

"No, Maurice, that will be all." Jamie said with anger in his voice! "I think Mr. Morgan and I are done here." With that he walked out of the room.

"Jamie, wait. Okay, right. That is real mature. Run out at the first hint of trouble."

Jamie came back into the room. "What is there left to say? You won't sell your ranch and I won't sell my family farm." Still raising his voice.

"Jamie, do you love me or was this just about sex?"

"How can you say that after what we promised each other?" Jamie was so angry and hurt at the same time. "I'm just going to ask this one more time Marc; do you love me enough to come here and live with me or not?"

"You aren't being reasonable, Jamie! The ranch is my life!"

"Well the farm is mine, so I guess that answers the question of 'is love enough?' It's not! I'll have Maurice help get your stuff ready for you and Keith to leave in the morning." With tears in his eyes he spoke again. "Goodnight and goodbye, Marc!" Jamie turned and left the room. He didn't look back and Marc didn't stop him.

Marc called Keith at the farmhouse and told him that they would be leaving early before daybreak. He and Jamie had completed the sale of Shadow the first night they arrived so there was nothing else to do but pack and leave.

"Keith, what's going on with our bosses?" Derek asked.

"They're fighting and the break up looks permanent."

"Does that mean that you and I aren't gonna be able to see each other when you go back to Cheyenne?"

"Of course not. Who cares what they do? We'll stay in touch and visit on holidays and vacations. Keith said.

"We had better make the most of tonight, Keith, because it will be awhile before I can come out to Cheyenne to see you." They moved in close and hugged each other.

"I loved having you here with me, Keith. Let's go up to my room and make love the rest of the night. Let our bosses fight if they want!

"I told you that Marc would never sell his ranch and move here. Jamie was fooling himself if he thought that."

"I know, but he loves Marc so much and he thought Marc loved him. too."

"He does — but he will not ever leave Cheyenne."

———————

Jamie watched from the bedroom window as Marc and Keith got their stuff in the truck. He had not seen or spoken to Marc since last night's conversation. "Why is he doing this? I thought he loved me," he thought as tears rolled down his face. His heart was breaking and there was no changing Marc's mind. "I can't leave my grandmother's farm; I was born here. There are too many memories to leave behind. Why can't Marc understand

that?" Jamie knew that the only way they could be together was if he gave up everything and moved to Cheyenne. "This is not fair, damn it! Why or *how* can he just
walk away from me?" Jamie asked the room. "God, I love
that man. I will always love him."

Marc looked up at the house and saw Jamie watching
from his bedroom. He could tell that he was crying but he
could not give in and move here. With tears in his eyes,
he looked one more time at Jamie and then climbed into
the truck. Keith gave Derek a hug and a kiss and told him
that he would call him when he got back to Cheyenne.
Just as they were about to pull away, Marc got out of the
truck and ran into the house and up to Jamie's bedroom.
He burst in the door; Jamie turned around from the window and stood still, staring at Marc. He couldn't take his
eyes off of Marc's lips.

Marc crossed the room and took Jamie into his arms
and begged Jamie. "Please don't let this be the end of
us. I love you and want you to be with me, always." They
both were crying now.

"I can't leave my home, Marc, and you can't leave your
ranch, so . . ." He couldn't stop crying long enough to say
anything else. It seemed hopeless. "If we love each other
we should try to work it out." Jamie said.

"Are you willing to move to Cheyenne for me?"

"No, I can't do it!"

Marc kissed Jamie and told him, "I will never ask you
again, but if you ever change your mind, you know where
I'll be." With that, he let go of Jamie and walked out of the

room and out of his life. Marc got in the truck and pulled away. He glanced back one last time. Jamie was not in the window this time.

Keith looked at Marc's sad but stern face and asked, "Can't you two work this out?" Keith saw a tear drop onto Marc's cheek as he shook his head.

"No."

CHEYENNE LOVE

Chapter Ten

The Book

Jamie tried to get back to life as usual. When he would go out to the stables to see Shadow and talk with Derek about how things were progressing with the horse, he would always know that if he asked about Marc that Derek would know. He and Keith were in touch every day. The problem was that he couldn't bring himself to ask; it still hurt too much.

Maurice would watch his boss with sadness in his heart. He knew he was hurting so badly inside. He wished he could talk to him about this because he knew how heartbreak felt. He remembered back when Jamie hired him: he was on extended service from England and didn't want to go back because his love had left him and never came back. He met Jamie and was hired immediately. That was three years ago. Jamie had become a successful and famous writer and needed a staff to manage his home. Maurice needed a place where he could work so he could stay in the states, so it worked out perfectly. Maurice's beloved wife of twenty-eight years had left him for another man and he had to get away from England. Working for Jamie had been the easiest job he had ever had. Maurice was given a staff of three to manage. Betsy, the cook; Hildegard, the maid; and John, the chauffeur. Maurice loved taking care of Jamie and his house. He had always been a generous and approachable boss. Living in Jamie's house had lessened the sadness and heartache after his wife left him, but every so often he would think about how much he loved her and still does.

———————

Everyone on the ranch knew that Marc was very upset. It had been only three months since he and Keith had left Berea, and he was barely speaking to anyone other than to give the staff orders. He and Keith, on the other hand, had talked often about Jamie, but Keith would never tell him what Derek was reporting to him.

Neither of the men had gone out with any other since the break up. After what they had together nothing else could compare. Marc had waited all those years for the right guy to come along, and now that he had, no one else would do. Keith and Derek discussed often about getting these two to give in and talk, but so far no luck. As each day and month passed, they were both still suffering so much, but remained very stubborn men.

Finally, Jamie finished the book he was writing about the beautiful, hunky Indian warrior named White Eagle. When he wrote about this Indian he patterned his looks after Marc. He kept his word to his true love and wrote the story about the Cheyenne warrior who falls in love but can never have his love.

All of the sadness Jamie felt for losing his love came out in the story of White Eagle. Many nights as Jamie was writing, tears would be flowing down his face. He missed Marc so badly that his whole body ached for him. Writing the novel, *Cheyenne Love* somehow helped ease the pain of his loss. When he sent it to his agent and publisher, they both read it and couldn't believe this love story. This book was so different from anything he had written, but they loved it. Jamie's agent asked who was the inspiration for the book. Jamie merely said, "Someone I will always love, but can never have."

Six months later, Jamie's book became a best seller and he had been traveling, doing book signings and talk show interviews. He also had been with movie producers about making *Cheyenne Love* into a movie. He was really happy these days with all of the traveling, etc. He didn't dwell on Marc so much, and what might have been. He would always love Marc, but it didn't hurt so much now. They say time heals all wounds and that is somewhat true, Jamie thought. He could pour all his love for Marc into making the book into a movie. It somehow brought him closer, but with less pain.

Keith came bounding into the house with a book in hand. "Marc! Have you seen or heard about this?"

"What is it?" Marc asked.

"It's a book called *Cheyenne Love* — and guess who wrote it?"

Marc's heart went into his throat and he felt he couldn't breathe. He looked at the gorgeous Indian on the cover and saw the author's name at the bottom of the page.

Written by Jamie Walker. He opened the first page and it read: *Dedicated to the man I love, always and forever.* Marc couldn't put the book down. As he read it, he cried. "God, Jamie, why do I have to love you? Why can't I get you out of my head and out of my heart? Is this ever going to pass, Lord?"

Two weeks later, he was watching the news and the announcement came on for the celebrities who would appear on David Letterman next, and he heard Jamie's name. He started to turn the channel but couldn't stand not to watch it. When Jamie came out, Marc could have died right there from lack of oxygen. He found he was holding his breath. "God, he looks more beautiful than before." All Marc could do was stare at the TV. "I want him so bad. He needs to be with me. This is where he belongs, in my arms." Marc picked up the phone and dialed Jamie's number. He knew that David Letterman is taped many days ahead. Jamie answered, "Hello?" ...a long silence. He knew someone was there. "Hello? Hello! Marc is that you? Please answer me!" Jamie heard a click and the line went dead. All the emotions he was trying to bury resurfaced in one moment. He knew it was Marc. He broke down sobbing. "Please, God, let me get over this!" he prayed and cried, but he knew he would never be free of Marc.

Chapter Eleven

A Chance

It had been a full year since the day Marc walked out of his life. They had not seen or talked to each other in all that time. "Cheyenne Love," the movie, was nearly finished. The last scenes were being filmed on location in Cheyenne, Wyoming. Jamie was very apprehensive about going to that location, but they needed him as technical advisor. Also, he was needed to assist the scriptwriter in transferring his book to the big screen.

"Derek, you need to be in charge here. I'll have to go to Cheyenne for the filming of the last part of the movie. The Hawthorns will be here to help you with the other chores around the farm. I don't know how long I'll be gone, probably a month. If you need anything, call me."

"Are you going to see Marc while you're there?"

"No, I haven't planned on it. I'll be so busy on the movie set and, besides, I'm sure he's moved on with someone else."

"No he hasn't, according to Keith. He's still carrying a torch for you. You know, he called you one time about three months ago but said when he heard your voice he couldn't speak. You both are such fools."

"Excuse me, what did you say?"

"You heard me! Why would you let geography keep you two apart? Both of these places are just houses, material possessions. What you two shared in the brief time together is worth more than a hundred farms or ranches. Like I said, Fools!!"

"You don't understand — this farm has been in my family since the Pioneer times, early 1800s."

"So what?!" Derek said loudly. "Do you think your Grandma would want you to lose the love of your life, — your soul mate — for a piece of property? I think not! Keith says the same thing to Marc. You two are throwing a love of a lifetime away, and it's a crime."

"Marc, did you know they're going to be filming "Cheyenne Love" here in Cheyenne and, according to Derek, Jamie will be here for about a month as technical advisor?"

"Are you serious? Do you know this to be a fact?"

"Yes. Derek wouldn't tell me this if Jamie weren't coming. I wish Derek was coming also but he says he has to take care of the place. He'll have a nice, elderly couple living at the farm helping him with chores while he takes care of the horses. I really miss him. We talk every day on email and sometimes on the phone, but that's no substitute for holding him in my arms and making love to him."

This whole conversation was driving Marc crazy. The thought of having Jamie that close and not be able to hold him would kill him. *How am I going to stay away from him if he's here in Cheyenne? I need him so badly. He's part of me now. He must be feeling the same. Can he really come to Cheyenne and not want to see me?* He couldn't shut his mind off. He decided that he had to know.

The first day of shooting took place in town by the train station. As they were running the scenes, Jamie sensed that Marc was there. He scanned the crowd of onlookers and then he spotted him. His heart stopped. He stood a distance away in that same black cowboy hat, black jeans and red shirt that he wore to dinner the night they first made love by candlelight on the bear skin rug in front of the fire. They stared at each other with love, lust and so many other emotions.

No! No! I won't let him do this to me again. Jamie couldn't stand it — he had to turn around and try to concentrate on the scene. *Why is he here? I can't concentrate with him here. Please go!* Jamie's thoughts were filled with so much sadness.

Marc watched him turn his back to him. He stood there a minute longer and then came to a decision. He started walking toward Jamie. When he got right up behind him, he leaned in and whispered in his ear, "Not this time." Jamie could feel his breath on his cheek and the heat coming from Marc's body.

"I want you, and I am not going to take no for an answer." Jamie slowly turned around to face Marc. He looked into those beautiful sapphire eyes and swayed.

He felt faint. Marc instinctively grabbed hold of him and pulled him the last few inches into him. "You are mine, Jamie Walker, and you will always be." He took possession of Jamie's soft kissable lips and forced his mouth open with his persistent tongue. They were both lost to the fact that they were in the middle of a crowd of actors, cameramen, director and onlookers. They didn't care. It had been a year since they kissed or even spoke to each other. When they came up for air, Marc said, "Please, Jamie, come home with me. I need you so much. You are the missing part of me. Please. I am begging you."

Jamie wanted this as much as Marc did, but would it change things? "Marc, I don't think we should do this."

"Then stop thinking and for once just be. I want you in my bed, I want to love you and come inside you, be with you. Please don't make me beg any more than I already have."

Jamie grabbed Marc on both sides of his cheeks and kissed him with so much passion that their audience hollered, "Get a room!"

Marc swept Jamie up into his arms and walked carrying him to the truck. He yelled back at the crew and said, "Mr. Walker will not be back for the rest of the day — and maybe not tomorrow, either!" Everyone watched in astonishment with smiles on their faces. Jamie wrapped his arms around Marc's neck and tingled all over. He was back in his true love's arms, and he was going to stay there if he could help it. He had yearned to be right here for the past year.

A Chance

Marc leaned down and kissed him quickly, softly and said against Jamie's lips, "I love you Jamie. Are you still in love with me? I have to know."

"Marc, I have never stopped loving you. I will always be yours, but you already know that if you search your heart. I gave myself to you completely and there will never be another man for me. Ever!"

Marc smiled that wonderful smile at Jamie, and Jamie was in heaven.

CHEYENNE LOVE

CHAPTER TWELVE

THE REUNION

When they were in Marc's truck, he said to Jamie, "Please slide over and sit next to me." Jamie did as he asked. Marc put his right arm around Jamie's shoulder pulled him close and kissed him again with fire and lust. Their need for each other was too overwhelming. Jamie moved his hand over to Marc's leg and on farther to his groin.

"Oh my god, Jamie, just you touching me again is going to make me come. I have built this up for a whole year, waiting for you." That was all Jamie needed to hear. He unzipped Marc's jeans and reached in for his target. Marc was hard and leaking pre-cum. Jamie bent forward and took Marc in his mouth. Marc moaned and moved forward for him to go deeper. Jamie licked and sucked and ran his tongue on the back of the shaft, driving Marc crazy. "I am not going to make it long." Jamie ignored him. He moved up and down for a few strokes then pulled off Marc and went lower, licking him at the base of his cock. Marc was moving and groaning and making sounds Jamie had not heard from him before. "Please Jamie, more…more…suck me hard and fast. I need you." Jamie complied and one more down to the base and up and Marc shot into Jamie's mouth. He didn't think he would ever stop and Jamie never missed a drop. As Marc was coming down off the most amazing blowjob, he told Jamie, "You wait till I get you home. I am going to slam so hard into you and you'll beg for more and more!"

Jamie zipped Marc's jeans up and stayed next to him in the seat. He didn't want to leave Marc's side for a moment. Marc had his right arm around Jamie and he held him tight. He was determined not to let Jamie go again. Jamie laid his head on Marc's shoulder. He was so content right now. Little did Jamie know that when Marc made the decision to come over and claim him, he knew if Jamie came with him he did not plan to let him go away from him again. Jamie was very quiet and Marc thought he might have fallen asleep in his arms.

All of a sudden, Jamie spoke; "What are we doing Marc? I still want you as much as ever, but us being together — making love again — will it solve anything?"

"Jamie, let's not talk about that right now. Let's just enjoy being together again. I've been aching to be next to you and holding you tight. I love you more than life itself and I know you still feel the same about me, too! You just demonstrated that quite nicely, I might add." Marc said with a grin on his face. Jamie looked at Marc's face and melted when he saw that grin and sapphire eyes dancing and twinkling at him.

"God Marc, I love you so much, sometimes I think my heart will burst." He nuzzled close to Marc's chest again, very content to stay there. Marc drove the short 14 miles to his ranch. Both men were very quiet but content. Marc pulled up the long driveway and stopped in front of the house. Jamie started to get out, but Marc stopped him. He bent down and claimed Jamie's lips once more. When they separated Marc told Jamie to let him get the door on Jamie's side. Jamie watched Marc walk around to his side of the truck and opened the door. Jamie climbed out and immediately was in Marc's arms.

"I love being in your arms again, Marc."

"Yeah, this is where you belong for always. We will work everything else out later but for now I just want to hold you and make love to you and show you how much I've missed doing this," as he came down to claim Jamie's lips again.

Keith saw them pull up and he couldn't wait to tell Derek what was going on here in Cheyenne. This was a good sign that they might be able to finally all four be together. Jamie started toward the door, but Marc stopped him and once again swept him up in his arms and carried him into the house. Jamie loved this possessive side of Marc. Once inside Marc put him down.

"Please Jamie come up to my bedroom with me and make mad, passionate love. I don't intend for us to come out for a long, long time."

"Marc, I have missed you every minute of every day."

"Me too! We belong together, not apart. This past year has been a waste and so sad. Come on, Jamie. Enough talking for now. I have other things that I want to do with you and talking doesn't figure in unless it's you telling me what you want me to do to you and the wonderful sounds that you make when I am inside of you. I have not been able to get those sounds out of my head for this whole past year."

Chapter Thirteen

Love for Always

They went up to Marc's room and closed and locked the door. Marc had given his staff strict orders that he and Jamie did not want to be disturbed unless they asked for something. He had already called them from the truck to send champagne up to his room. He planned to celebrate their reunion before they made love. The champagne was being chilled in his room when they arrived.

Marc poured Jamie and himself a glass and proposed a toast. "To us, together for always." Before they could even finish the drink they were in each other's arms again. Kissing, feeling and responding with their entire bodies. Marc pulled Jamie into a full body hug. Every inch of their bodies were in contact with each other. They could both feel the need between them.

"God Jamie, I have missed you more than you will ever know."

"Me too, Marc. You are all I've thought about every day for an entire year." Marc kissed Jamie again with so much love and desire. Jamie opened his mouth to receive Marc.

"I can't wait any longer Jamie," he whispered against his lips. He pulled Jamie over to his bed and started undressing him, first the shoes and socks, then the shirt. Once that was done he kissed Jamie on the neck, licking him down to his shoulder and back up his neck.

"You are so beautiful." He took his own shoes, socks and shirt off and then moved right up against Jamie again. They were chest to chest. He ran his hands over every inch of his chest, touching, kissing every spot, sucking and licking on his nipples and watching them get hard and erect. He loved running his tongue over and around them and watching Jamie's face. He could see how much Jamie loved that. Jamie was starting to breathe heavily and moaning with small, faint sounds coming from deep inside of him. Marc always loved the sounds Jamie made during their lovemaking. He sat Jamie on the bed and asked him to lay back. He proceeded to unbuckle Jamie's belt and unbuttoned his jeans, pulling them down and off along with his boxers. He stood at the foot of the bed and just stared down at Jamie.

God he is so gorgeous. He has the perfect body. Jamie laid watching Marc, then finally asked, "Are you going to stare at me all day or are you going to get undressed and join me?"

"I am not rushing this. I've waited to be with you again for an entire year." He started undressing the rest of the way and climbed in bed beside Jamie, pulling him back in his arms. Lying on their sides, their whole bodies were touching. The need for each other was so evident with both sporting full hard-ons. They pushed their groins together and rubbed up and down. Both were breathing heavily. Marc started kissing Jamie all over his neck, moving on to his chest, making sure to stop long enough to give both of his nipples attention on the way down to his waist, because he knew he would elicit those wonderful sounds that he gets from Jamie when he touches his tongue to his nipples. Jamie responded the way Marc knew he would. He sucked and licked on them, enjoying the feel of them in his mouth. Jamie was moving and bucking toward him, begging him to take him in his mouth, so he moved on following the line of hair down to his groin. He wanted to taste Jamie too. He took his cock in his mouth and could taste his pre-cum.

"Jamie, you taste so good." He sucked him, ran his tongue down the back of his cock and then down to the space between his shaft and his balls. He kissed and licked until he heard Jamie groaning. He moved back up and took him into his mouth and started moving up and down with a really slow movement. Jamie started begging him to stop or he was going to come. Marc ignored him the way Jamie had done in the truck. He wanted to taste every bit he could give him. It had been so long and he had been remembering and craving his wonderful taste.

"Marc, please stop or I won't be able to stop, Oh my god...too late! Marc!...Marc!" Jamie moaned in a deep sexy voice that almost made Marc come and he hadn't even gotten inside of Jamie yet.

"Jamie, give me all of it. I want this first." He moved a couple more times and received what he had been asking for and wanted. Jamie kept coming like he had never had an orgasm before. Marc took all of it and licked Jamie clean. Jamie was still coming down when Marc reached for some lube on the nightstand. "Jamie, I'm going to get you ready. I can hardly wait until I can be inside of you. Please spread your legs for me."

"No, Marc, I want to be on top with you."

"Okay, but I want to get you ready." He put lots of lube on his fingers and inserted them into Jamie. First one, then as he felt him relax, he put in another. He was moving his fingers in and out and finally felt Jamie was ready. He started to put on a condom but Jamie asked, "I haven't been with anyone since you, and you said you hadn't either, so do we have to use that? I want to feel you inside me with out any barriers."

"No, I'd much rather not use one, either." He prepped his cock with lube, but about that time Jamie stopped him.

"I get to be on top remember?" Jamie straddled Marc and impaled himself onto Marc. He was going to go slow, but couldn't control himself and sat right down with a force that shocked both of them. He sat still for a moment and then started moving up and down. Marc was going crazy. Jamie was the one in control and he loved having power over Marc. He got a good rhythm going and started driving both of them nuts.

"Oh my god, Jamie, you feel so good," was all Marc could get out. He was trying his best to not come too early, but Jamie was making him crazy. Jamie was hard again also, and Marc grabbed him and started working him up and down. He got into the same rhythm with Jamie and they were in heaven.

"Marc! Oh, Marc…I'm coming!" At the same time, Jamie stopped moving on Marc. Marc couldn't stand it; he started bucking his hips up slamming into Jamie. Two strokes like that and he shot his wad deep into Jamie. As he was coming, he told him that he had been going crazy without him. Jamie could barely speak, but he managed to tell Marc that it was the same for him. Jamie felt spent. He laid his head down on Marc, with him still inside. Marc's abdomen and chest were covered with Jamie's sweet love juice but neither seemed to mind. They were together again and neither wanted to let the other one go. A year is a long time to be apart but neither seemed to forget how the other felt during their lovemaking. It was like they had never been apart. Jamie was very content to lie like this forever, but Marc was getting soft and starting to fall out of Jamie. Marc lifted Jamie up and rolled him over onto his side. Cum was oozing out of Jamie and both were sticky and getting uncomfortable.

"What do you say we go take a nice hot shower and get something to eat?"

"Okay Marc, what ever you want." When Jamie got off the bed to go to the shower; he had remnants of Marc running down his inner thighs. Marc loved seeing that. He had his man back, and if he could help it he would never let him go again.

They showered and played with each other. Marc took Jamie back in his arms and hugged him while the water was running over them. He grabbed some shower gel and started washing Jamie all over. When he got to his groin, Jamie started moving and groaning and making those sounds that only Jamie could make. He was turning Marc on again just listening to him. He grabbed Jamie by the waist and turned him around to face the shower wall. Marc fingered him again but he didn't have to do much because Jamie was already wide open and ready. Marc placed his dick up against Jamie and slid in easily. He pushed in and out, closing his eyes and just feeling the tightness around him. He whispered in Jamie's ear. "You feel so wonderful I could do this all day and never get tired." Jamie just moaned. It was all he could do. He was so turned on that he couldn't put two words together. Every time Marc would push in and hit his prostate he would moan. As Marc was doing these wonderful things behind him, Jamie was stroking himself. Marc reached around and found Jamie's hand and put his on top. He started working with Jamie up and down; together they made Jamie spray the shower walls. Marc kept on moving in and out, hitting Jamie's prostrate with each stroke. He was driving Jamie crazy. Marc couldn't stop. All of a sudden, he pushed into Jamie as hard as he could, harder than he had ever pushed before, and caused Jamie to come again spontaneously, without any warning. That had never happened to Jamie or Marc before. Marc shouted at that same time, "I'm there, Jamie, my love! ...I'm giving you my love!" he said, as he came deep inside. He was so spent that he could barely stand. Jamie was holding onto the shower wall and swaying; his legs were like rubber. Neither had experienced anything that strong before. The hot water was making them both weak in the knees. Marc turned Jamie around and kissed him softly, and then helped him out of the shower. Jamie grabbed a towel, but Marc had other ideas. He wanted to dry Jamie off.

"Jamie, please let me do that." He took the towel and started drying him. When he got to his groin, he got down in front of Jamie and tenderly lifted his balls to dry them. The minute he did that, Jamie started getting a raging hard on again. Exactly what Marc had hoped would happen. He took him in his mouth and licked and sucked and kissed him up and down until Jamie gave him what he was so hungry for. Marc swallowed all of Jamie's wonderful love juice and licked him clean again. After this last bout of lovemaking, Jamie was unable to stand. Marc grabbed him and picked him up and carried him to the bed.

"Wow, I feel so weak Marc, you have to let me rest for awhile."

"I know, but it's hard for me to keep my hands and mouth off of you."

"You have to give me time to rest. I feel like such a weakling right now. What you do to me is driving me nuts!"

"I know, but I feel that I can't get enough of you! And I'm making up for all the time we missed this whole past year."

"Just lay with me for awhile." They got under the covers and just laid and held each other. Soon both had drifted off to sleep, locked in each other's arms.

CHAPTER FOURTEEN

LOST LOVE

The next morning, Jamie woke up first. He just kept looking at Marc, who was still sound asleep. "God, he is so handsome. How did I get so lucky?" Jamie thought. "We are so compatible in everything we do, but how are we ever going to make this work? One of us will have to give up our home...but which one?" As he was pondering this, Marc opened his eyes and looked straight into Jamie's beautiful, chestnut eyes.

"How long have you been awake?"

"Not too long, I was just studying your face so I can burn it into my memory forever."

"What are you jabbering about? You don't need to memorize my face, you'll see it everyday for the rest of our lives."

"You don't know that Marc! We still have this big problem to work out."

"What problem is that?"

"Oh, come on Marc, you aren't dense. The one of 'who gives up their home for the other?'"

"Are we back to that again? I don't want to talk about that now, I just want us to be together right now. We can work out the details of you selling your place and moving here later, much later" as he pulled Jamie close to him again. Jamie balked and pulled away.

"What are you saying? That I have to move here? What about you moving?"

"That is out of the question!" Marc said.

"You're telling me you won't ever entertain the idea?"

"No Jamie, I thought you understood when I brought you here with me that this is where you and I belong. I cannot leave Cheyenne."

That did it for Jamie. He got up and started getting dressed. "Where are you going? Don't tell me that after what we shared last night you're leaving me again."

Jamie didn't say a word, he just kept getting dressed. "Jamie, STOP!! Talk to me! Don't do this to us again!"

Not a word out of Jamie. Marc bolted from the bed and grabbed Jamie's arms. "STOP!! What are you doing? Talk to me." Jamie jerked his arms free and left the bedroom, ran down the steps and out of the house. He ran head on into Keith.

"Where are you going in such a hurry?"

"I have to get out of here. He did it again."

"He did what again?"

"He just assumed I would give up all I have and come here with him."

"Jamie, don't do this to him again. It will kill him. He loves you more than anything!"

"Well, obviously not. He loves this ranch more." Jamie said in tears.

"You are such a fool. You'll never find a love like

his again, and if you leave him this time, I'm not sure you'll ever be able to come back." Keith said pleading with Jamie.

"Well, so be it." Jamie said, so hurt his heart was breaking.

"Can I ask you a question?"

"Sure, I guess so."

"Do you love him as much as he loves you?"

"Yes, Keith, but I can't be dictated to and told where I will live."

"You and he are both unworthy of such a love. Derek and I would give anything to have a love half as good as what you two have and you're throwing it away." Jamie didn't want to listen anymore; he had to get out of there.

"Keith, will you drive me back to town? I need to get back on the set so that I can get far away from here."

"As you wish. I certainly will because you don't deserve his love. You're always running away; that's what you do best."

"How dare you talk to me like that."

"Why shouldn't I? What I said is the truth. You *don't* deserve him and after today I'm sure that you won't be welcome here again. He deserves to be with someone who wants him over every thing and every one else. That person is not you."

Jamie didn't look back at the house because it would kill him to see Marc again. Keith dropped him off at the movie trailer and neither spoke the whole way. Keith called Derek on the phone and told him what was going on with the "two idiots," as they called them.

The next day, Jamie was on the set and knew that Marc was nearby. He could feel him, but when he scanned the crowd he never could find him. The month went by quickly and filming was done. Jamie never ran into Marc again but always knew that he was close by, watching him. "I know I'm being stubborn," he thought. But he, for some reason, couldn't give in and it had become obvious that Marc was not going to change his mind, either. Jamie flew home. When he got there, Derek came to pick him up instead of John.

"Why are you here to get me? Where is John?"

"I told him I wanted to pick you up, because I'm going to try and get you to wake up and get back on a plane to fly back to Marc."

"I am not going back."

"Do you love him, Jamie, or are you just wanting sex with him?" Jamie swung back and punched Derek. The punch knocked him down, and right away Jamie felt bad for doing it. He reached out a hand to help him up. Derek was rubbing his cheek.

"I am so sorry for that Derek. I didn't mean it."

Derek laughed, "Well, at least I got my answer. You would not have hit me if I was right, so obviously you are in love with Marc, truly."

"Yes, Derek. I love him with all my heart."

"Well, he doesn't believe that. He told Keith that you obviously were not in love with him or you would not have left him again. He says he's done. He says it hurts too much, and he told Keith he couldn't wait for you any longer. He's going to try and get on with his life. Keith says he doesn't buy it, but that's what he passed on to me. Like Keith and I both said, you're both fools. You have a love that anyone would do anything to have and you guys just toss it away, like it means nothing. Such a shame!"

Jamie couldn't talk about it anymore. He rode to the farm in silence. *So, Marc is through waiting for me. He's going to move on. Okay, then so be it.* He was thinking all the way home. *I guess Keith was right when he said I would not be welcome there again.*

The movie debut was a great success. The picture was up for an Academy Award for Best Picture, Best Screenplay and Best Actor. Family, friends and everyone at the farm were so excited for Jamie. "Wow! An Academy Award!" everyone kept saying to Jamie, but he could care less. It had been months again since he left Marc's bed and he was still dreaming about being in his arms, remembering how he carried him off, how he made love to him in the shower until his legs wouldn't hold him. How he dried him off and put him to bed. How he woke up in his arms after a night of pure bliss. And here he was, alone and miserable. Keith had stopped reporting to Derek about Marc, so that made Jamie very anxious. *Is he with someone else now? Is that why Keith stopped reporting to Derek?*

One day about eight months after he left Cheyenne, he had gotten word that Marc was coming to the awards, per Derek, who got it from Keith. It made Jamie nervous. What would he say to him if he saw him?

Academy night came and Jamie was walking down the red carpet when he spotted Marc along the rope. He looked so handsome in a cowboy tux, all black. The sight of him took Jamie's breath away. He started to move toward him, when he saw this really handsome man come up to Marc and put his arm around him. Marc turned and smiled at his male friend. Jamie felt he couldn't breathe. He found he was holding his breath. They looked very cozy like they were definitely more than just friends. Marc saw Jamie watching them and smiled at him. Jamie decided the right thing to do was to go over to the ropes and say hello. He walked up to Marc and smiled and held out his hand.

"Hello, Marc."

"Hello, Jamie," he said as he took his hand. The electricity went all through Jamie. "I want you to meet my friend, Gary. Gary, this is Jamie Walker, the one I told you about who wrote *Cheyenne Love.*"

"Hi, Jamie, it's very nice to meet you. I'm really excited to meet a real celebrity." He smiled at Jamie with a smile that brightened up his whole face. Jamie thought he couldn't be any more perfect: blonde hair, baby blue eyes and long lean body. Gary immediately put his arm back around Marc, almost possessive of him.

Jamie looked back at Marc. "I am happy for you, Marc." He looked back at Gary, "Very nice to meet you." As he said that, he moved on down the red carpet and was being ushered to his place with the cast and staff of the movie "Cheyenne". "Good luck, Jamie!" Gary hollered after him, "We hope you win!" Jamie looked back and met dark blue eyes staring at him. Marc was watching him intently. "Why is he looking at me like that? God, I can't stand this. I never really believed he would move on, but I guess he has."

Jamie had a hard time concentrating on the ceremony, but when they called the movie as the winner, someone had to nudge him. He was so deep in thought and feeling like someone had punched him in the gut. He could barely breathe. He went up to receive his Oscar for Best Screenplay and didn't know what to say. He thanked everyone having anything to do with the movie, and then just as he was about to leave the stage, he said, "I would like to thank the man I love, who inspired me to write this story. He had never read one of my books, so I asked him what he would read and he told me 'stories about Indians.' Therefore, the idea for *Cheyenne Love* was born. I should be sharing this win with him, but that's not possible. I just wanted him to know that he had a lot to do with this story." Jamie then left the stage. Marc watched for Jamie to come back to his seat, but he didn't return. The ceremony was over and Jamie was nowhere to be seen. The crew cornered Jamie and made sure that he was going to the post-Oscar party. He didn't feel like celebrating, but knew he should put in an appearance.

He was standing off by himself when he felt someone behind him. He turned, and there stood Marc. "How did you get into this party?" was all Jamie could think to say.

"One of the cameramen invited me because he remembered me from that day of the filming when I carried you away. I just wanted to congratulate you on your win and to thank you for what you said up there. Even though I'm not that man anymore."

"Where's Gary?"

"He's in the men's room. Well, anyway, congrats!" Marc walked away and a few minutes later Gary joined him again.

"I have got to get out of here," Jamie thought and headed to the door. Marc watched him leave and felt like screaming at him: "STOP! YOU KNOW YOU STILL LOVE ME!" Instead, he stood silent.

Jamie caught the next plane out of LAX and was never so glad to be back home. Derek met him at the airport and asked how it went. Jamie told him about seeing Marc and his date. Derek gasped, "Are you sure they were a couple?"

"Oh, yeah. He had his arm around Marc and they seemed close."

"What did he look like?"

"He was gorgeous with blonde hair and baby blue eyes and a body that wouldn't quit."

"Could you tell if they were lovers?"

"No, but what else would they be? They sure didn't act like casual friends."

"I don't know, but Keith has never mentioned anyone like that to me.

CHAPTER FIFTEEN

HEARTBREAK

Things went back to normal pretty quickly. Horses needed taking care of and Jamie was busy writing again. He seemed really lonely and Maurice, Betsy and Hildegard were more than a little worried about him, because he was becoming a recluse. Hardly ever going out, and never any company. The three talked about what to do about Jamie. "How can we help him, Hildegard?" Maurice asked. He talked with Hildegard a lot because he felt very comfortable around her and, if truth be known, he liked her a little more than he felt he should.

Betsy spoke up, "I think we should try to talk Mr. Walker into letting the Hawthorns come back to help Derek with the farm, and Mr. Walker could go visit his friend in Cheyenne."

"We could try Betsy, but I don't think he would go. You know how stubborn he is. He thinks Mr. Morgan should come here." Maurice said.

"I know, but I don't think he will leave Cheyenne." Betsy answered

Hildegard chimed in, "Well, if he loves Mr. Walker then he should give in and come here. Maybe he doesn't love him like he says he does. I'm not sure he is good enough for Jamie!"

"Hildegard, what are you doing? You do not call Mr. Walker by his first name! Don't forget your place in the house!" Maurice reprimanded her.

"I know, it just makes me mad that the man Mr. Walker is in love with doesn't care enough to make him happy."

"You know, I think we should just stay out of it now that I think about it. We should let them work it out or not," Betsy said with fervor. "It's really not our place to even be discussing it." Maurice and Hildegard knew that Betsy was right.

———

Derek had been so busy with Shadow that he didn't come up to the mansion much anymore. Jamie tried to keep busy with his new book, but all he could think of was Marc.

When he did come to mind, he couldn't get the picture of him with the blonde out of his mind. *I have got to stop this! He has moved on and I should do the same.* Jamie stopped writing for a while and went down to the stables to see Shadow. He didn't do this often because seeing the horse made him feel worse, bringing back so many memories. Derek was there working with the horses.

"Hey, Derek."

"Hi, Jamie. It's really nice to see you down here. It's been almost three weeks since the last time."

"Well, you know why, I'm sure. The horse brings back too many memories. Memories I need to forget and move on with my life."

"Have you heard from Marc, Jamie?"

"No. Why do you think I would hear from him? He has a new love in his life."

"And who would that be?"

"You mean Keith hasn't told you about the gorgeous blonde, blue-eyed guy I told you I saw Marc with? I believe his name was Gary."

"No — he hasn't mentioned him at all and we talk every day." Derek knew who Gary was but couldn't tell Jamie because Keith said that knowledge would just hurt him more.

———————

Another month went by and Derek had some news that Keith wanted him to pass on to Jamie. Marc and Gary were going to have a ceremony to seal their relationship, even though they couldn't get married in Wyoming. Gary was going to move in with Marc at the ranch. Derek didn't want to tell Jamie this, but he felt he had to so Jamie would finally move on as well.

"Jamie, I have some news to tell you about Marc." Derek said

"What, is he hurt? Or worse?" Jamie was starting to panic.

"No. Sit down with me, please."

"What's going on? You're scaring me."

"Marc is going to sort of 'marry' Gary."

"NO! NO!! No, please tell me this is a joke." Jamie sunk down into the sofa with tears rolling down his cheeks. "Oh god, no…this can't be. Please tell me it is not so, Derek."

"Jamie do you really think I would tell you something like this if it weren't true?" Derek saw that Jamie was crumbling into a sobbing mess. He sat down with him and put his arms around him. Maurice came in about that time and saw the state Jamie was in. He looked at Derek and asked if there was anything he could do. Derek shook his head. They sat like that for the longest time until Jamie stopped sobbing and started getting control of his emotions.

"I never believed he would ever do this. I know he loves me, but I guess love isn't enough. You told me I was a fool and you were so right. I had the love of my life and I threw him away. Now someone else will spend the days and nights with him, and at some point I'll just be a distant memory of someone he once loved."

Derek knew there was nothing he could say at this point that would help ease the pain Jamie was going through. Wait a minute! "Jamie, have you thought about fighting for Marc? You know you could go there and try to reason with him. He would listen to you because I know he still loves you. He just thinks that you don't love him enough to come to him, so prove him wrong and go to him."

"It wouldn't change anything because I am still not willing to give him what he wants of me, giving up the only place I have ever known. Maybe this is for the best. He will have someone to love, who wants to live with him in Cheyenne."

Jamie walked out of the room and went up to his bedroom and shut the door. When he was alone, he started crying for the love he would never have again. "God, my heart is ripped from my chest and I'll never be well again."

Cheyenne Love

CHAPTER SIXTEEN

DECEPTION

"Keith, did you tell Derek the story about Gary?"

"Yes, I told him exactly what you told me, and he said he'd tell Jamie."

"I hate to deceive him, but I know this is the only way he'll move forward and hopefully find happiness."

"You must love him more than I thought, to forego your own happiness so Jamie can be happy."

Marc had asked his best friend from high school to pose as his new love. Gary said he wasn't sure he could pull it off since he is straight, but he wanted to help Marc and Marc had told him to follow his lead. Gary laughed and told him he would do that, but no kissing! "Don't worry, Gary, I don't want to kiss you, either!" They both laughed at how ridiculous this was going to be. After Gary met Jamie, he told Marc he was foolish for not telling him the truth. He said that Jamie could almost make him want to be gay.

"Yeah, he is gorgeous, isn't he?"

"Marc, why don't you just go to him?"

"You know why. You've always known since we were in school."

Jamie was still not talking to anyone at the house. He was basically staying in his room. He could not talk about Marc because every time he did he would lose it and start crying. He kept telling himself that he had to move on, but couldn't bring himself to do it.

He would always love Marc until he drew his last breath here on earth!

Derek had told Keith how badly Jamie took the news.

———•••———

The cold weather came. Advisories were out, and winter had arrived at the farm. All crops were turned over in the fields for planting in the spring. Derek was still busy with the horses, but not able to work them the way he wanted due to the snow and ice. This was definitely a quiet time for the farm. Winter had also come to Cheyenne. There was lots of snow on the ground at the ranch. It had been last spring since Marc saw Jamie and he yearned for him each day. He knew he did the right thing by having Keith lie to Derek about Gary. He just wished that he could have gotten Jamie to move here. They would have been so happy. "Oh well, I've laid down the path for Jamie and I to follow and it can't be changed now."

Time passed and Keith had to keep lying to Derek about Gary. He hated it, but that was the way Marc wanted it.

"Keith, can you get away for a week and come stay with me at the farm? I miss you so much. Please ask Marc for the time off."

Keith asked Marc and he told him to go. Things were

slow at the ranch and he really wanted news about Jamie. Keith took the next plane out and arrived in Lexington, which was the closest airport to Berea, then called Derek. Derek had already driven to Lexington and was waiting in baggage claim. Keith raced to get to Derek. He saw him first and snuck up behind him, wrapped his arms around his middle and kissed him on the neck.

"Hi, my love." Keith whispered to Derek.

Derek turned around in his arms and kissed him longingly. "I have missed you *so* much, Keith."

"Me too, Derek." They got Keith's bag and went to the truck. Inside the truck they kissed again and then headed out to the farm. "How is the farm and Shadow?"

"All is well there."

"How's Jamie?"

"He's not good. He's not eating well and he hardly ever comes out of his room. He just stays up there and writes his novel and pines for Marc. ...Speaking of Marc, how are him and Gary doing? Are they happy?"

"Derek, pull over a minute. I want to talk to you and I want your full attention."

Derek was worried when he said this, but he did what he was told to do.

"Ok, what? You have my attention."

"Gary and Marc are not together, married or otherwise."

"But, you said . . ." Keith interrupted him.

"Yes, I know what I told you. But it was all a lie, so Jamie would move on and find someone else to love and make him happy."

"That isn't going to happen because he hardly ever comes out and I know that Marc is the only one he'll ever want to be with. When you love someone like Jamie loves Marc, no one else will ever take his place. Why did Marc do this, and who is this Gary?"

"Gary is a friend of Marc's from high school. He agreed to do this charade even though he's straight. He cares about Marc, so he agreed."

"Well, that answers that, but *why*? Did he really want to kill Jamie?"

"No, this was totally selfless on his part. He knew that after all this time Jamie was never going to change his mind about moving, and Marc can't move. So nothing else could be done. He hoped if Jamie thought he had moved on, then he would too and finally be happy."

"God, these two are killing me." Keith pulled Derek into his arms. "Aren't you glad we don't have these problems?"

"Don't we? We aren't living together either, and we should be."

Keith listened to what Derek was saying and was curious as to what he was feeling, so he asked him to spell it out. "Why, do you think we should be living together Derek?"

Keith held his breath while he waited for Derek to answer.

"Because I,...uh,...I...I'm in love with you." That was the first time Derek had ever said this to Keith. Keith hitched his breath.

"You are in love with me?"

"Yes, you fool, how could you not know?" Keith leaned in and kissed Derek long and sultry. When he pulled away, he looked softly into Derek's hazel eyes and said, "I'm in love with you, too. So what are we going to do about it?"

"Well, first when we get to the farm, I'll show you how much I love you and then we should talk about our plans. I want to be with you and I am not going to be stubborn like Jamie and Marc."

When they got to the farm, they disappeared into Derek's bedroom and locked the door. They spent the rest of the day and night making love and making plans. Derek was going to have to tell Jamie that, at some point soon, he would be moving to Cheyenne to live with Keith.

The next day, Derek and Keith were out in the stables to check on Shadow. Jamie couldn't stand it; he wanted to hear any information about Marc. When Jamie walked into the stables, Keith whispered to Derek to keep the secret.

"Hi, Keith, how are you doing? I know Derek is so glad to have you here. ...How is Marc?"

"He's real good. Not very busy right now, so he has a lot of time on his hands." Jamie didn't want to ask the next question, but he couldn't stop himself.

"Is he happy with Gary?"

"Yes, Jamie, he seems to be." Derek wanted to scream *It's a lie!*, but he knew what Marc had done for Jamie was the best for him, given the situation. The whole week Keith was there Jamie tried to come down to the stables everyday. Maybe Marc would call Keith about something and he could ask to talk to him.

"This is crazy," Jamie said silently to himself. "I'll call Marc." Jamie picked up the phone and dialed Marc's number. He didn't know why he felt the need to talk to him all of a sudden, but he chalked it up to seeing Keith again. The phone rang three times and Marc answered. "Hello?"

"Hi, Marc." When Marc heard Jamie's voice tears formed in his eyes and he was a little choked up.

"Hi, Jamie, how are you?"

"I've been fine, Marc, thanks for asking." This small talk was hurting both of them so much. Finally Jamie had to ask. "How's married life treating you and Gary?"

Marc wanted to tell Jamie the truth but knew that nothing had changed. "It's been fine, Jamie."

Jamie listened to the way Marc sounded when he answered him. "Just 'fine' Marc? Not great?"

Marc was silent. This lying was too hard. "Yes, just fine. After all, Gary is not my first love and they say you never get over your first. Look, I'm sorry to cut this short but Gary and I have a dinner engagement to go to. It was nice talking to you, and tell Keith to get home soon." Marc hung up and sat down on the floor and sobbed. *I love him more than life. How can I keep going like this? I need him with me. Why did he have to call? I was good until I heard his voice.*

Jamie listened to the dial tone for what seemed like minutes. *Why did I call him? I didn't want to hear that he's happy with Gary. There's nothing to be done.*

Deception

Keith had to go back because his vacation was over, but they made plans for Derek to come to Cheyenne after the spring crops were planted. Derek was not going to tell Jamie for a while yet. He noticed that Jamie was even more withdrawn after talking to Marc. Jamie and Marc were definitely star-crossed lovers. So sad.

Cheyenne Love

CHAPTER SEVENTEEN

THE ACCIDENT

Keith filled Marc in on how bad off Jamie was. "He is not moving on like you thought he would. This lie is destroying him slowly, one day at a time. Please Marc, tell him the truth. Your plan did not work. He isn't eating good, or sleeping, and he looks gaunt. He literally is grieving himself into an early grave. You have to help him."

"It's only been a few months; he will get better."

"You're not much better." Marc knew Keith was right, but how could he do it?

Keith was out riding one of the stallions that Marc was going to sell to a buyer from Texas. Things were fine at first, but the path was a little icy and snow covered and he didn't see the rise in the ice. His horse lost his footing and fell with Keith still on his back. Keith's head hit a rock and knocked him out. The horse was lying on Keith's right leg and couldn't get up. When Keith didn't come back, Marc got worried and went out looking. He found them on the trail. He checked Keith and he was still breathing but was not conscious. He immediately called 911 and then tried to get the horse off of Keith.

The horse was still flailing about, trying to get up. Marc noticed that the horse's leg was broken badly. He was going to have to be euphemized because the break was too bad. He got on the phone again and called the Vet who takes care of his horses. The EMTs got there fast and attended to Keith. One of them helped Marc get the horse off Keith. When they finally got the horse up, he couldn't stand and went back down again. This time, though, the EMTs had pulled Keith free.

"You take him on to the hospital and I'll wait here with the horse for the Vet. Then I'll come. Please take good care of him."

Marc's Vet came and agreed that the horse could not be saved. "You go on to the hospital and check on Keith. I will take care of this."

"Ok. I'll call you later to make arrangements for the horse." Marc sped to the hospital. When he got there they had Keith in Nuclear for CT scan and MRI of his skull to assess the damage. They were sure he had a skull fracture, but were worried about pressure to the brain. He had not come to yet. That worried them, also. They put him in ICU and hooked him to a heart monitor and had an IV going. He was exhibiting signs of hypothermia, so they had him under a warming blanket to bring his body temperature up. Marc looked at all the equipment hooked to Keith and got really scared. He sat down next to his bed and held his hand while talking to him. "Keith, please open your eyes." It had been several hours now and the doctors said the longer he goes without waking up, the worse it could be.

Suddenly there was a flicker of his eyes. He spoke one name: "Derek." He spoke it again, and then he slipped into a coma. The doctors raced in and asked Marc to leave the room for a minute. They wanted to assess him. Keith's doctor came out and told Marc that if he had any family, he should call them to come at once. They weren't very hopeful. Marc knew that Keith didn't have any living relatives, so he called Derek.

"Derek, this is Marc!"

"Hi, Marc, what is it? Do you want to talk to Jamie?"

"No, I need you to listen, Keith has had a bad accident and he's in really bad shape. You need to get here as soon as you can."

"What do you mean? He is going to be okay, right?"

"No, Derek. He's in a coma, and they don't hold out much hope. He called out your name twice and then slipped into the coma. Please get here as soon as you can."

"How did this happen?" Tears were rolling down Derek's cheeks.

"I'll tell you that when you get here, just please come now. He needs you here."

Derek got off the phone and called the airport. He booked the first flight out to Cheyenne. He ran up to Jamie's house and told him what was going on. "How bad is he?"

"I don't know, but Marc says I need to come now. He's in a coma and the doctors are not giving much hope."

"What? Well go, I will figure out something here. When you get there let me know what is going on, please."

Derek packed and John drove him to the airport. Jamie called the Hawthorns to see if they could come take over the duties at the farm.

Derek arrived at the hospital within five hours from Marc's call. When he walked into the ICU and saw Keith, he almost passed out. He was so pale and swollen and bruised, with IVs and lines coming out all over. One whole side of his head was disfigured where he hit the rock. Derek started crying and sat down beside him, took his hand and leaned over to kiss his lips. "Keith, I'm here baby, please wake up and talk to me." He stayed there, holding his hand and crying for hours. There was no change in his condition.

Marc came back in and asked him to come out for a while because he wanted to tell him what happened. Marc told Derek that the horse slipped on the ice and went down, trapping Keith under him. They got the horse up and off him but had to put him down. Keith was conscious some of that time and was calling Derek's name. The doctors told Marc that when he slipped into a coma it was a bad sign. Possibly the pressure on the brain had increased, so they were monitoring him very closely. They had hopes that he would come out of it, but as time went on it was looking very grim.

Derek called Jamie to fill him in. Jamie felt so sorry for Derek. He knew Derek loved Keith. Derek sat day after day holding his hand and talking to him. Telling him to please wake up and love him. Finally, after two weeks of being in a coma, while Derek was talking to him Keith blinked his eyes. When he opened them completely, he saw Derek and squeezed his hand. "Oh my God, Keith, you scared me. I thought I was going to lose you!" Keith was very weak, but he smiled at Derek and in a soft voice, "I love you, too."

Marc came in when he heard the nurse say that Keith was awake. When he got to Keith's bed, he leaned down and hugged him slightly. "You had us all worried sick. We can't run this ranch without you." Keith started to say something but couldn't get it out. Alarms started going off, his heart rate started climbing, doctors and nurses were running into the room ordering everyone out. They called a "code blue." Keith was crashing. Marc and Derek were pushed out. Keith was non-responsive. Derek was screaming his name and Marc had his arm around him, trying to hold him from running back in the room. The staff worked on him a few minutes and then finally his doctor came out and told them they had stabilized him but needed to take him to surgery now to relieve the pressure off his brain. The doctor told them to wait in the surgery waiting area and he would come out when they were done.

Derek was so scared. He couldn't lose Keith. While Keith was in surgery, Marc and Derek talked about the future. Derek told him that he and Keith had decided that he would move to Cheyenne and live with Keith. "Have you told Jamie this news?"

"No, not yet. We were waiting until all the necessary arrangements were made and of course I'll need to give Jamie plenty of notice for him to replace me." Marc couldn't stand it he had to ask. "How is Jamie? Does he have someone to love him now?"

"You're kidding, right? He will never have anyone because he's too much in love with you. He's told me that he intends to spend the rest of his life alone."

"He shouldn't do that. He should find someone who can love him and stay with him in Berea to make a life."

"Marc, you're kidding yourself. He will never get over you like I'm sure you've gotten over him." Derek was angry now because Keith was fighting for his life and he and Derek want to be together and Marc and Jamie are throwing what they had away. This whole thing was not fair. Derek started to say something else to Marc, but the surgeon came out into the waiting area at just that time. The look on the surgeon's face was heavy. Derek didn't wait for him to speak. He screamed and fell to the floor, sobbing, "NO! NO! NO! PLEASE, GOD, NO . . ."

CHAPTER EIGHTEEN

DECEPTION NEVER PAYS

"Stop. He is not gone. He is still alive." The doctor helped Derek up from the floor and sat him down on the sofa.

"But your face — you looked so sad, I thought . . ."

"I'm sorry! We relieved the pressure on his brain but he's still in critical condition. His vitals are still way too high and he remains in a coma. I am not going to sugar coat this: he is still in danger of not making it. We need his vitals to stabilize and for him to wake up. I am going back into recovery. He will be back to his room in an hour."

"Derek, let's go down and get something to eat." Marc led him down to the cafeteria. After they ate, he did feel better. They got back up to the ICU just as they were bringing Keith back to his room. Derek grabbed Keith's hand and kissed it and begged him to come back to him.

Derek spent the next eight hours sitting right by Keith's bed. He just kept talking to him about what they were going to do when he moves here. Marc stayed with Derek at the hospital. The next morning things started looking better. Keith's vitals had come back down to normal. He was still not awake, but Derek was encouraged that he may make it after all. Marc had come in to relieve Derek for a while. Derek went to the ranch and showered. He told Marc he would be back in an hour.

Marc started out to the nurse's station to get some water, when he ran straight into Jamie. Marc was speechless. Jamie found his voice first. "Marc! How is Keith? Is Derek in his room, I'll go on in, if that is okay!"

Marc was still having trouble finding his voice. He couldn't stop his heart from racing at the sight of Jamie, and his mouth was so dry. "Well, the least you could do is say Hello, Marc." Jamie was hurt and mad because Marc wouldn't even speak to him. He started to brush past him and go on into Keith's room, but Marc grabbed his arm to stop him. Jamie jerked his arm away from Marc's touch. Just his touch was bringing back so many memories.

"Jamie — I'm sorry, it just took me by surprise when I saw you! Derek is at my ranch taking a shower. He'll be back soon, and Keith is still in a coma. Please come on into his room." That was all he could manage to say. Being this close to him and not being able to pull him into his arms was killing him. He wanted to shout, "I love you still and forever!" but he couldn't do that.

Jamie went on into Keith's room. He sat down next to the bed and took Keith's hand. He bowed his head and said a silent prayer for him to wake up. Marc stood at the door and just watched Jamie. He still couldn't believe he was here. Derek came up behind Marc and touched him on the shoulder. "What are you doing standing in the door?" Marc just nodded his head toward Jamie.

"Oh my god, Hi Jamie." He said as he ran into the room.

"Hello Derek, how are you holding up?" He gave Derek a big hug. A wave of want and jealousy ran over Marc when he watched them hug. "He didn't wake up while you were gone. I am so sorry Derek." Jamie and Derek walked out into the hall to talk.

"The doctors say that the longer he stays in a coma, the worse it could be. God Jamie, I can't lose him, I love him so much."

"You need to have faith that God won't take him away from you." Derek went back into Keith's room. Jamie stayed out to give Derek his privacy with Keith. He sat down in the waiting area. Marc followed him and sat down.

"How have you been, Jamie? I heard you're writing another book. What is this one about?"

Jamie looked up to look Marc in the eyes, "It's about a lost love." He said very matter-of-factly. That statement really hurt Marc because he knew that it was probably about them. He felt he had been kicked in the gut, and the nonchalant way Jamie said it caused him to hurt even more.

"How is Gary?" Jamie asked, even though he really didn't want to hear that they were happy.

"He's doing fine," Marc lied. He knew he had to keep up this sham.

"Where is he? I would have thought that he would be here with you to support you."

"He has to work, so he gets the updates when I go home at night and when Derek goes back to take a shower and sleep for a little while."

Something seemed off with Marc's manner. He was too vague with his answers. Jamie felt he wasn't telling him the truth, but how could he find out what was going on with Marc? *Why do I even care?* he thought, but he did care and wanted to know. He came to a decision and thought he would go with it. "Marc, I was wondering if I can stay at the ranch with Derek, so we can catch up. It would be easier if I were there...if you don't have a reason why I shouldn't," he added when he saw Marc's face. He looked like he was going to jump out of his skin.

"Uh...no...there is no reason why you couldn't stay at the ranch." Jamie knew by his actions and the scared look on his face that he was hiding something. "Maybe he and Gary are not as happy as he would want me to believe," he thought.

"I promise I'll stay out of your and Gary's way. You won't even know that I'm there."

Marc was in a panic. *Now what? And was Jamie kidding when he said I wouldn't even know he was there? I feel him even if he is not next to me! God, what I am going to do? Gary isn't even in town right now so he can't even come over and pretend. What am I going to do?* He stood up and started pacing back and forth. Jamie really knew that this antsy behavior of Marc's was very suspicious. "I will find out what's going on here before I leave," he thought.

Derek came out of the room and walked straight up to Jamie. "Did you book a hotel room before you came to the hospital?" Derek asked.

"No, Derek, I just asked Marc if I could bunk at the ranch with you." Derek jerked his head around to look at Marc. They exchanged this weird look, giving Jamie even more to go on. Something is definitely off here. *What are they hiding?* He would find out before he goes back home. Jamie got up and asked Derek if he could go back in to see Keith.

"Sure." Jamie got up and walked directly in front of Marc coming very close on purpose. Marc sucked in a breath and Jamie heard it. *He's still bothered by me when I get close. Why is that?* If Marc were happy with Gary, why would he still be able to get this reaction from him? He disappeared into Keith's room.

"What are you thinking, Marc? Jamie can't stay at the ranch; he'll find out your secret regarding Gary. Then what? You never should have made up this sham. It never pays to lie. It will come back to bite you in the ass and it looks like that's exactly what's going to happen here."

"I know...but what was I going to give as a reason why he couldn't stay with us. He knows I have a very big house." Marc sat down and put his head in his hands. "God, this is going to blow up in my face, isn't it?" Derek just shook his head and said, "If you're going to continue with this facade, you'd better call Gary to see if he can come back or Jamie is going to find out the truth!" Marc knew he was right so he made the call. Gary answered right away with concern in his voice, as he knew Keith was in the hospital and was afraid it was bad news. "Hello, Marc — please tell me Keith isn't gone."

"No, he's still in a coma, but his vital signs are improving."

"Well, how is everyone else doing?"

"Gary, can you make a quick trip? Jamie's here and I told him he could stay at the ranch."

"What? Are you nuts? Why did you tell him that? Never mind. You're going to have to come clean, Marc, because I can't get back for a few more days. I'm sorry."

"I can't tell him the truth!"

"Well, you'll have to come up with something then. You know, he's going to find out sooner or later so just get it over with and tell him."

"Some friend you are! ...Just kidding, Gary. I know you'd help if you could. I'll see you in a few days."

"Tell him, Marc!"

———

Jamie sat down next to Keith. He took his hand and started talking to him. Keith tightened his fingers in Jamie's hand, which got Jamie's attention. "Keith. Keith, open your eyes please. Can you hear me? If you can, squeeze my hand." Keith squeezed his hand. Jamie jumped up and yelled for Derek to come at once. Derek ran into his room, "What? What is it?"

"He's coming to. I was talking to him and he moved his fingers." Derek took the seat away from Jamie and started begging Keith to open his eyes. Derek bent forward and kissed his lips and softly whispered, "I love you." Keith slowly opened his eyes and was having trouble adjusting to the lights, so Jamie turned the overhead lights off so that it wouldn't bother him so much. That helped, and he started trying to open them again. He looked at Derek and told him in a whisper that he loved him, too.

Marc went to get the doctor and they came back into the room. "Well, Keith, welcome back from your long sleep. I need to check you over real quick and then you can spend time with your friends." The doctor listened to his chest and performed a complete Neurological exam. All was good, he reported to the room. Keith was trying to say something but was having trouble verbalizing. Derek leaned in close and put his ear to Keith's lips. "I am very hungry, my love." He said. Derek laughed and hugged him.

"What did he say?" Jamie asked.

"He says he's very hungry!" The doctor said they would have to start him on clear liquids and then they would see. Keith made a face. Everyone in the room laughed. Derek leaned over and kissed him again. "We are so glad you came back to us. I am so glad that you came back to me. I could not have gone on without you." Keith was very weak but he smiled at Derek. "I love you so much" Keith whispered. At that, Jamie and Marc left the room so they could have their time together.

"Well, I guess Derek will stay here with Keith tonight, so I'll go and check into a hotel." Jamie told Marc. "I only wanted to stay at your ranch to catch up with Derek but now I'll do it later." He went up to the nurse's station to get a phone book. He was going to stay at the Plains Hotel which he remembered was the great historical hotel they stayed in while filming "Cheyenne Love." He wrote down the number and went over to sit on the sofa and make the call to get a room and then a cab.

"Stop, Jamie. I told you that you could stay at the ranch. It's silly for you to stay at a hotel when my house is so big." Marc had no idea what he was doing. He should have let him go to the hotel because that would solve his problem about not letting Jamie know that he'd lied, but he wanted him close to him.

Jamie was hoping that Marc would stop him. He took a chance by saying he would go to a hotel, but he was determined to find out what was wrong here. "Okay, Marc, if you are sure that I won't be in the way with you and Gary."

"No, it will be okay. Gary won't mind." When Marc said that it felt like Jamie had been stabbed in the heart all over again. "I don't know if I can do this," Jamie thought.

CHAPTER NINETEEN

DISCOVERY

Jamie climbed into the truck with Marc and sat right up against the passenger door. He couldn't stand to be even this close to Marc. He wanted so badly to scoot over and wrap his arms around him, but he knew he was not his anymore and he would not welcome this jester. So, he stayed where he was in silence.

Marc was very much aware of the turmoil that was going through Jamie. He, too, wanted to just get close to him and pull him into his arms and never let him go again, but he knew that Jamie was no longer in his life and with the deception he had started he had no right to take this step. His biggest concern now was how he was going to cover up the lie about Gary. "Why did I do this to both of us?" he wondered. Just being this close to Jamie was driving him crazy. He is so in love with him.

They rode to the ranch in total silence. When they pulled into the drive, Jamie's heart started pounding and he felt he couldn't breathe. He never thought he would be back here again. "How am I going to do this?" He thought. When the truck stopped, Jamie jumped out right away. You would have thought the seat was on fire, the way Jamie got out. He knew he was acting stupid, but he couldn't stand to be in that close of proximity with Marc. Marc walked around the truck to get Jamie's suitcase out of the back. Jamie reached for the case at the same time, running headlong into Marc. They were actually so close that they could feel each other's breath on their cheeks. Marc looked into Jamie's eyes and held his gaze. He then moved one step closer and he was right up against Jamie. Their bodies were touching. "What is Marc doing?" Jamie thought. "He looks like he's ready to kiss me. I'm not moving...he'll have to move first." Jamie knew this was stupid to stand his ground, but if truth were known, he loved being this close to Marc again.

Marc leaned his head down and barely touched his lips to Jamie's. Jamie leaned in to meet Marc's lips and kissed him back in that instant, but then pulled away quickly. "What are you doing Marc? Don't you care about Gary seeing you kissing me, or do you have that little of respect for me to do this when you're a married man?"

"I'm sorry Jamie, I have no excuse. I guess old habits die hard." He turned away and walked into the house. Jamie grabbed his bag and followed him in. When they got inside, Marc told his housekeeper to put Jamie's suitcase in one of the guest rooms and told Jamie to follow him into the parlor. Marc's butler came in and asked if they would like something to eat and drink. Marc told him to bring two beers and fix a steak dinner for two. They would eat in a little while. He turned back to Jamie and said, "Please make yourself comfortable on the couch. I'll check on your room and be back in a second."

"Marc, are you going to tell Gary that I am here? Why did you say only dinner for two — isn't Gary eating with us?" Marc stopped dead in his tracks. His mind was racing but he couldn't figure out what to say.

"Yes, he'll eat with us. I guess I'm so used to saying 'two for dinner.' I'll correct it with my cook and go find him. We'll be right back." Marc left the room.

Jamie still thought that Marc was acting very funny. "Why would he forget that it would be *three* for dinner? Something is just not right. I guess I'll know more when I see Gary again and watch them together."

Marc got outside of the room and thought: *Okay, what do I do now? I'm going to have to come clean I think, but he will really hate me then. I just can't tell him now. I'll think of something.* He went upstairs to his bedroom and paced around for a few minutes trying to kill time. Meanwhile, Jamie was walking around the parlor muttering, "What's the big mystery, and why did Marc kiss me? I saw the want and desire in his eyes when we were standing right against each other. God, how I wanted him to take me in his arms and hold me. ...Jamie, you have to stop this! Marc is not yours anymore."

Marc came back into the parlor. "Jamie — Gary sends his regrets but he's really sick and in bed. He thinks he has the flu so he won't be joining us for dinner. I told him to stay in bed and that I would be up later if he needs me."

"Oh, I am so sorry he's not feeling well. Tell him I hope he's better tomorrow." Jamie was glad that he was not going to join them. He was looking forward to being alone with Marc.

They sat down across from each other drinking their beers. The tension was so thick you could cut it with a knife. Neither knew what to say to each other. Jamie wanted to get up and pull Marc out of his seat and beg him to take him in his arms. Meanwhile, Marc was wishing that he had not told Jamie the lie about Gary. He wanted him so badly.

Finally, Jamie asked, "What was the next step with Keith? Now that Keith is awake, when will they let him come home?"

"I don't know, but I am sure that Derek will keep us informed. What are your plans, Jamie? How long are you staying?" His mind told him he should hope that Jamie will not stay long, but his heart screamed "Stay with me Jamie, always. I love you and always will."

Jamie didn't know if Marc wanted him to leave by asking this question, but he would not stay any longer than he needed to. He can hardly stand the stress of being around Marc.

"I'm leaving in the morning. I'll go to the hospital to see Keith and to tell Derek that I am going home."

Marc felt like someone punched him in the gut. *God, why did I make up this lie? Well, now you're paying the price for your deception. Jamie is in arms reach and you can't touch him.*

Chase (Marc's Butler) came in and told them dinner was ready. Jamie followed Marc into the dining room.

Marc was sitting at the head and Chase had Jamie sitting at the first place to Marc's right. Chase poured the red wine and served the steaks. Marc and Jamie sat in total silence as they ate. Jamie was wondering why it felt so strained being with Marc. They were acting like total strangers instead of ex-lovers.

All of a sudden, Jamie brushed against Marc's leg with his leg and both men froze. The connection was instantly causing problems for Jamie; his jeans were getting very tight and uncomfortable. Marc did not make a move to pull his leg away. He was totally letting the connection last. He wanted more contact with Jamie than just this. Jamie didn't move, either. Marc stopped eating and sat back and looked at Jamie, watching the expressions in his eyes changing with every second that their knees were together. Jamie also stopped and stared back with the same longing and intensity that was in Marc's eyes.

Chase came back in the room to see if they wanted any more wine and broke the spell that had engaged both Marc and Jamie. Jamie moved his knee away from the contact leaving Marc feeling the emptiness right away. He wanted that contact back. "Aren't you going to send some food up to Gary?" he asked Marc.

"I'm sure that he doesn't feel like eating anything right now." Chase looked at Marc with a questioning look that passed between them. Something is just not right here. Then it hit Jamie that maybe Marc was lying to him. He would not stop until he finds out what's going on. They finished their meal and took their drinks back to the parlor. Jamie sat down on the couch close to the fire. Marc noticed how beautiful Jamie was with the glow of the fire dancing off his face. Marc stayed standing with his foot on the hearth just watching Jamie out of the corner of his eye. Jamie noticed how sexy Marc looked standing there and wanted him even more than earlier. *I have got to stop this. He is not mine anymore.*

"Marc, I'm going to go up and say hello to Gary. I'm not afraid of getting the flu — I 've had my flu shot." And with that statement, he headed towards the door.

"No—" Marc said louder that he meant to. "No, you can't go up there." Jamie kept walking. Marc closed the distance between them with two steps and grabbed Jamie's arm.

"Why don't you want me to go say hello to him?"

"I just don't want him disturbed. Maybe he'll feel better in the morning and you can see him then." Jamie could see the panic in Marc's eyes, so he stopped and started to remove his arm from Marc's grasp, but Marc wasn't letting go. Instead, he moved in closer. Jamie could feel the body heat and his heart started beating faster. *What is he up to now? Oh God, he's going to kiss me again. I want this...I want this, but I shouldn't let him.*

Marc moved swiftly before Jamie could pull away and pulled him in the rest of the way. He kissed him with all the passion that a lover who was starving would do. Marc moaned against Jamie's mouth and forced Jamie to open and let him in. He was no longer holding back, he wanted Jamie and he couldn't stop this. Jamie was melting into Marc and wanted this as much as he did. They both could feel the want and need between them, their bulges in their jeans left little to wonder. They were both ready to strip and fall on the floor where they stood to satisfy their longing and love for each other. It was very clear now to Jamie that regardless of Marc's situation, they still were very much in love with each other. Nothing had changed. They couldn't keep their hands off each other. Marc was pushing Jamie back to the couch and had all intentions of making love to Jamie right there. He pushed Jamie down and fell on top of him. "I want you now Jamie. I can't go another minute without having you as my own." He was kissing him on the mouth, neck and ears. Jamie suddenly came to his senses and pushed Marc off of him, causing him to fall to the floor. Jamie jumped up and headed for the door.

"God, Marc! How can you be so crass and unfaithful to your marriage. You are a bastard and I am glad we didn't marry. You'd probably be unfaithful to me, too."

Marc was stunned at Jamie's words, but he knew why he was saying these hurtful things. *He really believes my lie.*

Jamie stormed up the stairs to his room and closed the door, telling himself, "This was a bad mistake coming to stay here with Marc. I can't control myself and he obviously can't either." He decided to go to Marc and Gary's room and tell Gary how sorry he was and hoped that he would be able to forgive Marc this small mistake.

He knocked on the door to Marc's room and waited. No response! He opened the door and went in to talk to

Gary. He expected to find him in the bed, but the bed was made with no sign of Gary. He walked into the bathroom to see if he was in the shower, but no one. "What is going on here?" He sat down on the bed to try and sort this out. Being in there brought so many wonderful memories of their lovemaking back to Jamie and he couldn't help it — he laid back against the pillow with his eyes closed, remembering. Oh, how he loved Marc and still does. "What is he trying to do to me, making me want him again? And where is Gary? Why did he lie to me about Gary being sick up here?" Jamie was deep in thought with his eyes still closed. He didn't hear Marc come in.

Marc moved very quietly to the bed and just stood watching Jamie. *He knows now that Gary is not here. I'm going to have to tell him the whole story, but will he listen to me or run away, the way he has always done?*

CHAPTER TWENTY

TIME FOR TRUTH

Marc sat down on the side of the bed and Jamie's eyes flew open, but he didn't move. "What's going on here, Marc? Where is Gary?" Marc put his finger to Jamie's lip to stop him from talking.

"I have to tell you the truth now, Jamie. I never expected you to come here again so I never thought I would have to tell you. Are you willing to listen and not say anything until I am done?" Jamie nodded his head. Marc started talking. "First thing you need to know: I am still *so* in love with you. There has never been anyone else and never will be."

Jamie said, "But..." Marc stopped him again.

"You agreed to listen until I am done. There was never a Gary and I am not married. Jamie started to protest and move but Marc stopped him. "Please, Jamie, listen to me. I made up the whole story and made Keith and Derek go along with it. I wanted you to be able to move on and find someone to love who could be happy living with you in Berea. That person is not me. I thought that if you thought I had moved on, then so would you. Gary is my best friend. We grew up together all the way through high school and college, and he is straight. He agreed to do this for me because I convinced him that this was for you. He always thought I was crazy, especially after he met you at the Awards. He thinks we belong together and no one else will ever satisfy us. He is so right there. I will never be with anyone else. I love you more than this ranch, my life, everything — but I cannot move away from here and I have very good reasons that I have not shared with you. I did this because I want you to be happy and live a full life with love. I don't want you to be alone for the rest of your life like I intend to do. I had not been with anyone before you and I will never be with anyone after you, so you were wrong when you accused me of being unfaithful. I will always be faithful to you until my last breath here on earth."

Jamie was crying at this point and could not even see Marc's face for the tears. "Well, Jamie, now you know the truth and I'm sure you will never forgive me for putting you through this heartache. I heard it from Derek how much you were suffering, but I still felt it was for the best since neither of us can give in to the other." Marc got up off the bed and left the room. He could not stay another moment in there with Jamie on his bed. He wanted him so bad and just ached for him.

Jamie stayed there for the longest time trying to take it all in. He was feeling so many emotions: anger, relief, heartache, love, sadness, yearning, anger again, understanding. They all went through him, and he began asking himself, "What should I do? Can I forgive him for all these months of heartache and longing for something that I thought was gone? Jamie, what do you want? Are you willing to let Marc go away from you again?" As he spoke, he closed his eyes and beyond his control fell asleep in Marc's bed. Hours passed and Marc waited for Jamie to come downstairs but he didn't. Marc decided to go check on him. He first looked in Jamie's room, but he was not there, so he went to his room and quietly opened the door. He found Jamie in his bed asleep on top of the bedspread. He walked over and thought that he was by far the most gorgeous man he had ever seen. He just watched him sleep for a few more minutes and then decided he should wake him up so that he can go to sleep in his own bed. He was pretty sure that Jamie would not want to share a bed with him. He shook him a little and Jamie opened his eyes. Marc could have lost his soul in those eyes staring back at him.

"Jamie you've been asleep for a while, so I think you should wake up now and go to your own room. I promise I will not bother you."

Jamie stared at him for the longest time and then asked him, "Marc, is that what you want me to do, go to my own bed?"

Marc just about lost his composure. *What is Jamie doing, trying to drive me crazy and make me suffer the way I caused him to suffer?* When he got over the shock of what Jamie was asking him, he came back with, "No, you know that is not what I want. I want you to stay here in my bed with me, but I know how you must feel about me now, so I would never ask you to stay. Tomorrow you will be back at your farm and that will be the end of it."

Jamie ignored that and asked the same question again. "Marc — is that what you want me to do, go back to my own bed?" At that comment Marc reacted. He sat down on the side of the bed and bent down, pulled Jamie into his arms and kissed him passionately and completely. Jamie responded by kissing him like he could not get enough of him, either. Marc pulled Jamie's shirt off and started kissing him on his neck, ears, and chest. Jamie was in heaven and had no intentions of stopping him. Marc stood up and pulled his clothes off and then unbuckled Jamie's pants and with one movement had them off so both were completely naked. He moved to the other side of the bed and laid down, pulling Jamie's naked body to him. Jamie was hard and ready to have Marc make love to him. He had come to the decision to let the hurt go and let the love come back between them. He wanted Marc and no one else.

They kissed and kissed until both of them had swollen lips and they wanted it all. Marc took Jamie into his mouth first to give him the pleasure that he had been storing up for him. Jamie moaned and bucked and was not too far from coming. "Please, Marc, make me come." Marc went all the way down and sucked and hummed against Jamie's hard dick until he couldn't hold back anymore. He shot his load in Marc's willing mouth. Marc had been craving the wonderful taste of Jamie for so long. He took every drop. It was quick, but it had been so long since they were together.

Marc was hurting himself at this point, so he grabbed himself and started working himself. Jamie stopped his hands and pushed Marc on his back. He moved quickly and positioned himself between Marc's legs. "Now it's my turn. He teased Marc a little by licking down his shaft and back up, putting his tongue on the slit at the top, getting a good taste of Marc's wonderful juices. He loved the taste of his love and missed it so much. He had yearned for it so many nights alone in the dark. Marc was moaning and begging Jamie to take him all the way in. Jamie opened his mouth wide and went all the way down on Marc, at the same time caressing his balls and moving his hand back to Marc's opening. He came off Marc's dick and went down between his legs, licking him around his opening. Marc was making noises that Jamie had never heard. He could tell that Marc was going to shoot his load and he didn't want to miss that, so he took him back in his mouth. Marc grabbed Jamie's head and fucked his mouth until he screamed, "I'm coming!" Jamie sucked and swallowed and licked him clean. Marc was coming down and he pulled Jamie up to kiss him.

"Oh my God, Jamie, I always thought our lovemaking was great — but this was unbelievable!" He held Jamie in his arms until they both came down and were quiet again.

"Jamie, I want you to know that I love you and will always love you no matter what happens from here." Jamie listened quietly to Marc and tried to decide what he wanted to say.

"Marc, I have to say this just once and then I will not say it again. You really hurt me when you let me think you had moved on with Gary. And then when I heard you were married, I wanted to die. I even thought about ending it all. I now know the truth and I do understand your motive. I had to tell myself that the important thing in all of this is that you *are* still mine and I love you — so I cannot hold this hurt any longer. I forgive you, but please don't hurt me like that again. I wanted to wait for a while before we made love again but when you come near me I can't stop myself. I will always want you — and only you — to make love to me and grow old with me."

Marc couldn't stand it any longer, he pulled Jamie to him and kissed those kissable lips until neither one could breathe. "Marc, I want you to come inside of me and make me yours again for the rest of our lives." Marc didn't need to be asked twice. He wanted this, too. It seemed so important to both of them. He got some lube and started preparing Jamie. It had been a very long time for them both, so it was like starting all over again which was okay with both of them: slow and easy. When Marc started pushing into Jamie, Jamie started crying causing Marc to stop, frightened that he had hurt him.

"Jamie? What's wrong? Did I hurt you?"

"No... Marc, please don't stop. These are tears of happiness."

Marc leaned down and kissed Jamie tenderly and whispered against his lips. "I love you Jamie Walker, for always." He pushed all the way in and started moving slowly at first, but Jamie wanted him hard and fast. So he was bucking into him, causing Marc to totally loose control and pounded him into the mattress. Both came at the same time, Jamie spurting spontaneously from the whole lovemaking session and Marc exploding deep into Jamie. When they separated they just laid in each other's arms, mess and all. They didn't care. Both were so happy that if they moved it might end the happiness. They clung to each other and fell asleep totally exhausted and happy.

Cheyenne Love

CHAPTER TWENTY-ONE

THE SECRET

The next morning, Marc woke up first and stared at Jamie in his arms. He started thinking about what Jamie said last night about how he was almost tempted to end it all when he heard about Marc marrying Gary. He lay there thinking, "God, if my lie would have caused him to do that, how would I ever be able to live another minute? You are so stupid and selfish. You really don't deserve his love." About that time, Jamie opened his eyes and saw that Marc was crying.

"What's wrong? Aren't you happy that we're together again?"

"Oh, Jamie, yes! But I was thinking how close I could have come to losing you forever."

"What are you talking about?"

"You told me you thought about ending your life over my stupid lie."

"Hush, Marc. It's over, and I am still here."

"Yes, but how can you be so forgiving of what I did?"

"I told you — I decided to give up the hurt and let the love come back. I am just so happy that you're still mine and belong to no one else! So stop and kiss me." Marc pulled him in and kissed him over and over.

"We should get up and shower, eat some breakfast and go see Derek and Keith." Both got cleaned up and ate. They had decided that they would talk about where they go from here later. When they got to the hospital, they found Derek lying in bed with Keith and both were asleep. Jamie went out to the nurse's station and asked if Keith was still doing okay. The nurse told Jamie that he had a good night and would probably be able to go home in a few days. Jamie went back in and told Marc. They went out to the waiting room to wait until Derek and Keith woke up. While they were out there, Marc decided that he should finally tell Jamie why he couldn't move away from his ranch.

"Jamie, I want to tell you something else that I have not been able to share with you."

Jamie got a worried look on his face but didn't say anything and let Marc talk.

"I know you've always thought I was being stubborn all this time by refusing to move to Berea with you. The fact is I *cannot* move — not that I didn't want to but I can't. What I'm going to tell you is very private and the only ones who know are my best friend Gary, Keith and my house staff. I have a twin sister who lives with me at the ranch. She is in a totally separate wing in the house."

Jamie interrupted Marc and said, "Why didn't you tell me you have a twin and why haven't I met her? Why do you keep her a secret, especially from me?"

"Hush, Jamie, and I will tell you. When Mary and I were 18 years old, we were out riding and it was slippery and her horse went down, pretty much like Keith's did. Only she wasn't as lucky. She cracked her skull on a rock and never came out of the coma. She's still in the coma after all these years. Our father brought her home finally, when the doctors said they could do no more for her. They said she might stay in this coma until her body finally quits and shuts down, or she may wake up anytime without warning. Before my Dad passed away, he made me promise that I would never sell the ranch and he wanted me to always keep her here with me and to never put her in a nursing home. So, you see why I can't come to live with you. I want to be with you more than you know, but I can't sell the ranch and break my deathbed promise to my Dad."

"Marc, I'm speechless. Why didn't you tell me this? Why would you hide her from me? You have to know that I would never hurt her."

"Yes, I know that, but my pride kept me from telling you. I thought that you should want to be with me enough to leave your place and come here with me and I didn't want Mary to be the reason. My ego — or pride, or whatever — was driving me to stay silent about her."

"Are you ashamed of her or what? I really don't understand your keeping this from me. Did you ever think that if I had known sooner it might have saved us all this separation?"

"You were so set on staying at the farm for your own family reasons that I didn't really think it would make a difference." Just as Jamie was about to say something else, Derek walked out into the waiting area.

"Hi guys, I am happy to report that Keith is going to be just fine! They did another neurological test on him last night and he still has no deficits. His memory is intact and he should be able to come home in a few days. I can hardly wait to get him all to myself!"

"That is great, Derek." Jamie said. Marc looked at Derek.

"What are your plans going to be when Keith comes home?"

"Well, I guess that this is as good a time as any. Jamie, I'm moving to Cheyenne to be with Keith as soon as the spring crop is planted. So you will have to hire a new farm hand and groom. We're in love, and we're not going to be as stupid as you and Marc are about not being together!"

"Well Derek, you should know that I'm aware of the deception, and I also know the reason that's been keeping Marc here, so I have some decisions to make myself." He smiled at Marc, who had a shocked look on his face, the same as Derek's. "What? Why are you two looking at me like that?"

"Soooo! Does this mean what I think it means? Do I dare hope what you are planning?"

Derek chimed in at that point, looking from Jamie to Marc and back. "You two have gotten back together, haven't you?"

Marc walked over to Jamie and pulled him in close. "Yes, we are back together and I might add better than ever." He noticed Jamie blushing at that and tightened his grip on his waist.

"Wow! Wait 'til I tell Keith. He'll be so happy! Derek went back into Keith's room. Marc turned Jamie to face him.

"Are you really thinking about coming to live here with me?"

Jamie reached up and kissed Marc and just shook his head. Marc pulled Jamie in tight to him and told him that he was going to love him and hold him and never let him go. They just stood and hugged. Wrapped in each other arms.

"You know, Marc, that there is a lot to do and I want to see Mary. God, she must be beautiful — a female version of you. Wow!"

"She won't know you're there, but if you want we will do that later today."

"You don't know what she hears. She may have been hearing you talk to her all these years."

"I've sat for hours when you left me, just telling her how sad I was. For some reason it made me feel better talking to her."

"Between my meeting her, bringing Keith home and going back to the farm to decide what needs to be done there, it's going to be a busy few weeks or maybe months."

"I know I don't need to ask you this, but I will anyway just to hear you say it. Will you wait for me to get my personal affairs in order?"

Marc took Jamie in his arms again and whispered against his lips. "No way!"

Jamie pulled back and looked at Marc sadly. "What? You won't wait for me?"

"No, because I am not letting you go away from me for any amount of time!"

"But?" Marc silenced him with a kiss. "I am going with you. You will never get to far from me again. Ever!"

CHAPTER TWENTY-TWO

SWEET MARY

Marc and Jamie left Derek with Keith at the hospital and told him they would be back later. Marc wanted to take Jamie home to meet his sister. They went to Mary's wing of the mansion and Marc told her nurse that she could take a break while he and Jamie were there. When they walked into her bedroom, Jamie's breath caught in his throat. Looking at her face was like looking into Marcs; their features were identical. She looked so peaceful, like she was sleeping. Jamie thought of fairy tales he used to read to his little niece. She was definitely a sleeping beauty.

Marc went up to her side and leaned down to kiss her on the forehead. "Mary, I want to introduce you to someone. This is Jamie. I told you about him. He is my love, my future."

Jamie sat down in the chair by her bedside and took her hand in his. "Hi, Mary. I am so glad to meet you. I want you to know that I love your brother more than life itself and I promise to make him happy from here on until we both leave this earth. I would love to come talk to you everyday from now on, if that would be okay with you. I'm going to go to my farm in Kentucky and make arrangements to move here with your brother, so I'll be away for a short while. But when I come back, we'll get to know each other." He bent forward and kissed her on the head just like Marc did. They stayed with her for a little while and then left her. "God Marc, she is beautiful. She's like looking at you only with feminine, softer features."

"Now do you fully understand my not being able to leave Wyoming? I can't send her away from here. This is the only home she has ever known."

"Yes, Marc, I do get it. What I still have a little trouble with is that you didn't tell me your reason. Your silence on this matter has caused us a lot of wasted time that we could have had together. Your reason for staying here is far more important than mine is for staying at my farm. Yes, my farm is important to me because it's been in my family for generations, but that's a silly reason compared to yours."

"I told you my ego wouldn't let me tell you. I thought if you loved me enough, then there shouldn't even be a question."

"Well, I felt the same about you. I felt if you loved me enough you would move with me. We were both very stupid but enough said about this. We need to make plans now. Keith is not going to be able to take care of things here, so I will leave Derek here to help you with the ranch and horses. I will go home and settle the farm and ship my horses here. I also need to figure out..."

"Whoa, Kentucky boy. I told you — I am not letting you out of my sight! We'll go back to Kentucky together and work on the arrangement together, as a couple."

"But, what about Derek and Keith? They probably could use your help."

"No. I talked to Keith's doctor this morning and he said that except for some cuts and bruises, he should be able to resume his work slowly in a day or so. He said that Keith was very lucky to have no problems after all that he had been through. Derek said not to worry because he would take care of things. So, as soon as we get Keith home and settled, we'll leave for Kentucky." Jamie just stood there looking at Marc. He was thinking, "I never thought I could love this man anymore than I already do, but I do."

Marc looked at Jamie and said, "...What?"

Jamie moved up to Marc and wrapped his arms around his neck. "I love you more than words can say, Marc Montgomery Morgan" as he softly kissed him.

"Stop or we won't get to the hospital."

———————

"Keith, do you believe that Jamie and Marc are done being stubborn and Jamie is moving here?"

"I am so glad that Marc finally told Jamie why he couldn't leave Cheyenne."

"What do you mean 'told him'? What is there to tell? Jamie had to finally give into Marc because Marc was not about to give..."

"No, Hon, you're wrong. I can tell you why, now, because Jamie knows the whole truth." As he told Derek about Mary, Derek felt so bad about what he had been thinking about Marc. "Wow! No wonder Jamie decided to sell and move here."

———•·———

Two more days went by with Marc and Jamie making love every night and plans every day. They would be leaving for Kentucky on Friday. Keith was coming home today and Derek was walking on cloud nine. He was finally going to be able to hold Keith in his arms, naked, with no nurses looking at them. "Keith, when I get you home, we are going to my bed and I promise I will be gentle with you but I need to have you in my arms."

"That is where I want to be more than anywhere I can think of."

Derek, Marc and Jamie brought Keith home and Derek immediately kept his promise by taking him up to his bed. Jamie and Marc knew they would not see them for the rest of the day. Around dinner time they came back down to join Jamie and Marc. The four sat down to dinner and talked over what was going to happen in the immediate future. Derek and Keith were so happy that Jamie and Marc were finally together. They talked about what needed to be done here. Most of the work would have to be done by Derek because Keith was still not up to par, but he could supervise him as to what he does with the horses. Derek told him he was used to working with horses and Keith laughed, "I know you are but let me feel like bossing you around a little." They bantered back and forth playfully, loving being together again.

Jamie and Marc made their arrangements to fly out in

the morning to Kentucky and told the other two that if they needed them to call immediately. All four retired to their rooms...well, not quite. Keith went to Derek's room and Jamie went to Marc's.

Derek wanted to give Keith some rest since he kept him busy all day. "You go to sleep, my love, and I will be with you when you wake in the morning."

"I am pretty tired. I love you Derek" and drifted off to sleep. Derek whispered in his ear, "I love you back."

————

Chase came up to Marc's room to announce that Gary was downstairs. Marc replied, "That's great! Tell him we will be right down."

"Are you sure I should go down with you Marc? Maybe you should talk to Gary alone." Jamie wasn't sure how he felt about Gary. He knew the deception was Marc's idea, but how could Gary do this to someone knowing it could be hurtful?

"No Jamie you are coming with me." They both went downstairs. Gary was in the den, waiting. When they walked in Gary turned around and Jamie again thought what a gorgeous guy he was.

"Hey, Marc, Jamie! I heard the news from Chase. I'm glad you finally know about Marc's deception and I'm truly sorry about my part in it, Jamie. I hope you can forgive me as well. I told Marc all along that he was being foolish but he felt it would help you to move on." Jamie stood still for a moment and sized Gary up. He seemed sincere. Marc and Gary did not know what Jamie's silence meant, and they were hesitant to say anything else. Jamie finally moved toward Gary and held out his hand. Gary took it and shook it.

"Gary, I am glad to see you again and this time I would like to be your friend too." He smiled at Gary and Gary smiled back.

"Marc you are a very lucky man!"

"That I do know, Gary," Marc said as he pulled Jamie to his side.

Jamie continued, "I thought I was angry at you, Gary, but like I told Marc, I'm letting the hurt go. If he had to pick anyone to be 'married' to, I am glad it was a straight guy and not a gay one!"

All three burst into laughter.

"I would love to be your friend, Jamie." Gary said, smiling from ear to ear. When Gary left them about an hour later, Marc and Jamie retired to their room.

"It is so good to have Keith home and well. Those two will be very happy together, and so will we."

Jamie and Marc made love until both could hardly move. "Marc, I love you, but you are going to have to stop because I am so tired, and sore by the way!"

"What? Can't take too much of a good thing?"

"Go to sleep. I love you." Jamie said. "Night." They fell asleep holding each other.

Chapter Twenty-Three

Selling the Farm

Early the next morning all four met for breakfast and talked about the next couple of weeks. Keith told Marc not to worry about anything at the ranch; with Derek here and Gary back in town, he knew they would be fine. Jamie and Marc were driven to the airport to settle things in Berea. When they arrived at the farm, the Hawthorns greeted them.

"How is Keith?" Mrs. Hawthorn asked.

"He's great, thanks for asking. Well, I want you guys to be the first to know that I am selling the farm and both houses and moving to Cheyenne with Marc. Oh, by the way, let me introduce you. Mr. and Mrs. Hawthorn, this is my boyfriend and love, Marc Montgomery Morgan."

"It is a pleasure to meet you Mr. Morgan. We have heard a lot about you from Maurice, Hildegard and Betsy. They were kind of mad at you for not moving here with our Jamie."

"Please call me Marc, and I can just imagine how they felt. Nice to meet you."

"Yeah, well Marc had a really good reason for not moving here, so I am moving to be with him. I will contact a realtor, but in the meantime, if you know anyone who might be in the market for a farm, let me know. Derek is not coming back, so can you guys stay until I get this sold?"

"Sure Jamie, we love it here." Mr. Hawthorn said.

With that, Marc and Jamie went out to the barn to see about the horses and to see how Shadow was holding up without anyone walking him on a daily basis. They found he was just fine, so they moved on up to the main house. Maurice was waiting for them.

"Hi, Mr. Walker." Hildegard stepped forward. She and Betsy were waiting for their cue to go back to work.

"Betsy, please cook us up a good, homemade fried chicken dinner with all the works. Mr. Morgan here eats way too much beef. Oh, and before you all go back to your duties, let me tell you what's going to happen. I'm selling the farm and moving to Cheyenne with Marc. Now before you start worrying about your jobs, Marc and I talked about how we could keep everyone on staff from both households. Maurice, you would be in charge of the whole staff; Hildegard you will work alongside Marc's two maids as equals; and Betsy, we want you to come run the kitchen and help feed the ranch hands in the bunk house. Marc's cook will work for you because you are more experienced. Are there any questions?"

Maurice spoke up, "Mr. Morgan don't you already have a man servant?"

"Yes, Maurice, but he would rather drive for me and not be in charge of the house. He says the maids give him headaches."

"I know how that feels," Maurice said as he looked over at Hildegard.

"Yes, I am sure you do." Marc said. My man's name is Chase, by the way. You would be in charge at double your salary. That goes for you also, Betsy. Hildegard, you will get a sizeable pay raise."

"Oh my god, Oh my god, yes, yes, yes!...That sounds great!" yelled Hildegard. She was so happy that she hugged Jamie.

"Hildegard!!" Maurice yelled at her. "What do you think you are doing?"

"It's okay, Maurice, she's just happy." Betsy just stood shaking her head at Hildegard in disgust. "She is a loose cannon," Betsy thought, but she loved her all the same. They were all very excited.

"Well, guys, I haven't heard a 'yes' from anyone but Hildegard. Do you accept our offer to come with me to Cheyenne?" Maurice was trying to stay dignified when he spoke, "Yes sir, I would love to come with you, and thank you Mr. Morgan."

"We second that" said Hildegard and Betsy.

"Okay then, that part is solved. Now, to deal with the hard part — selling the farm. How am I going to do this? I've lived on this farm my entire life." This was going to be so hard for Jamie.

Marc watched the pain come across Jamie's face, because this farm is all he has ever known. *It's breaking my heart watching him give up his homestead, but I don't know how else we can do this. I feel like I am being selfish.*

"Jamie, can I talk to you privately?"

"Sure Marc, what's the problem?"

"Jamie, are you sure about leaving your farm and all that you have known here? If you're not sure, then we need to decide what to do."

"Yes Marc, it is going to be very painful to leave this place but now that I know you can't come to me, there is no choice. I want to be with you for the rest of my life and like Derek told me one time a very long time ago, my grandmother would not want me to choose a house over my true love. She would want me to be happy and I can hear her now..."*Jamie, you should never give up the love of a lifetime just because of a house. Yes, there are a lot of memories here but you will always remember them and now you are supposed to make new memories with your true love.*"

"My grandmother was a very smart woman, so I need to listen to her voice in my head." Marc walked over to Jamie and took him in his arms. "I just want to hold you and tell you that I will always love you and will do all that is humanly possible to make you happy."

"I know that, Marc. That's why, even though this is hard for me, it's the way it's suppose to be. I want to spend the rest of my life showing you how much I love you."

It was late when they finally retired to the den to drink some coffee and plan out what they had to do tomorrow. Jamie stood in front of the fireplace sipping his coffee. Marc stood back and watched him. He knew he was sad and he understood it. He walked up behind him and put his arms around his waist and pulled him back to him. He kissed him on the back of neck and whispered in his ear. "Jamie, I am so in love with you. I know you are sad. I hate that this is hurting you."

"Stop, Marc. What would hurt me more is not having you with me for the rest of my life. Yes, there are a lot of memories here for me, but we will make our own memories together. That is more important."

"I do know what you are sacrificing for me."

"Now that I know you are mine and always have been, it is no sacrifice."

"Jamie, I have something for you that I wanted to give you that time I came to see you at the movie filming in Cheyenne, but the way things ended I never gave it to you. I want you to have it now." He pulled out a jewelry box and handed it to Jamie.

"What is it?" Jamie asked.

"Open it and see." Jamie opened the box and inside was an ID bracelet in 18 carat gold with *Jamie and Marc* engraved on the front. Inscribed on the backside, *"I am yours and you are mine, forever. Love, Marc."*

Big tears were rolling down Jamie's face. "Oh Marc, how beautiful. You have kept it all this time?"

"Yes Jamie, I couldn't bear to get rid of it. God, how I love you." With that he picked Jamie up and carried him upstairs to Jamie's room where they first made love. They undressed each other very slowly and when they were naked in each other's arms, they took things very slow and tender. They wanted this night of love making to be even more special, like their first time in this room. Marc lifted Jamie up again and carried him to the bed.

"No, Marc, stop." Marc froze. "What is this now, oh god, no!"

"No...No... it's not bad," Jamie assured him. "There's a fire going and the bear skin rug is still here." Jamie gave Marc a sweet innocent look that melted Marc into submission. Marc got the hint; he moved them both to the rug and pulled Jamie down beside him. "Is this what you want, my love?" Marc kissed Jamie with all the longing of a man who has been without his love for such a long time. Even though they had made love over and over since the night Jamie forgave him, they had not made love here where they first consummated their love. "Jamie, have I told you how much I love you and thank God every day for bringing you to Cheyenne to check on Keith and Derek? If you had not come to see them, we may never have come back together and we would have lost the only love that either of us could ever want."

"I know, Marc. I love you, too, and feel like the luckiest man in the world because I have your love to be with me always. They spent most of the night making passionate love until both were so satisfied and surrendered to sleep.

"Marc — Marc, wake up" Jamie was shaking him. "What?" he said still half asleep.

"Wake up, I just had a perfect solution to the farm."

Marc rubbed his eyes and looked at the animated face of Jamie. "What are you so excited about this early in the morning? You know you kept me up most of the night making love to you and then you wake me up at the crack of dawn."

"Oh, hush your belly aching. You know you wanted to make love to me most of the night. I didn't have to twist your arm." Jamie grinned at him and that was all it took. Marc pulled him into his arms and gave him a very thorough kiss.

"Now, what were you saying?" He smiled at how disoriented Jamie was after that powerful kiss. "What's the matter, can't you talk now?" Puffing up his chest at Jamie.

Jamie wrestled him back down on the rug and sat on top of him. "Now who has the control, Mr. Morgan?" Marc looked up at the satisfied look on Jamie's face because he knew that he had him right where he wanted him. "I think you had better get off of me or I will not be responsible for what I do to you next."

"Promises, promises." Jamie said as he got up to run away to the bathroom. Marc was hot on his trail. He grabbed him and pushed him up against the bathroom door. Do you want to surrender now or after I have my way with you?"

"How about after you have your way with me." They were having fun playing but when Jamie said that, Marc could not stop himself and he kissed Jamie's lips and forced him to open up for him. Jamie opened his mouth to let in Marc's luscious tongue and moaned when their groins rubbed together. "Marc, please take me now." Jamie was Marc's to do as he pleased and he pleased a lot. Marc wanted to take him right where they stood, so he lifted Jamie up and wrapped his legs around his waist. He put his fingers in Jamie's mouth for him to lubricate them and then started preparing him. Jamie was wide open and ready for Marc. Marc entered Jamie hard and fast but both were so hot at this point that Jamie didn't even protest the roughness, in fact he was getting hotter by the rough way he was being taken. Both worked together to satisfy their need for each other. Marc started moving faster and faster until he came deep inside Jamie. He was breathing so hard that he could barely catch his breath. He slowly slipped out of Jamie and Jamie started taking his legs from around Marc's waist. He was a little shaky but Marc held him tight as he got his balance. Marc started kissing Jamie again and licked down his neck, around his rock hard nipples, sucking and flicking his tongue against them. As he moved farther down he noticed that Jamie was so hard it looked like he might break. Jamie moaned and tried to move his hips toward Marc but was a little too shaky. Marc held him still and moved on down and took Jamie into his mouth. He worked him so gently at first but Jamie started moving with him and wanted it faster. Marc sucked and licked up and down his shaft until he heard Jamie's breathing catch and he knew he was going to taste the wonderful love juice of Jamie. Jamie came and filled Marc's mouth...Marc never lost a drop. He came back up and held Jamie tight to him.

"Wow, I didn't wake you up for this but I am sure glad you thought I did. When we get cleaned up I would like to tell you what came to me in the night." Both got in the shower and washed to get ready for the day.

"What did you want to tell me?"

"I'll tell you at breakfast. Lets go eat."

"I already had a little morsel this morning." Marc said with a wicked smile as he walked Jamie downstairs.

"Oh, you think you are so cute, don't you?"

"What? And you don't?" Marc said as he patted Jamie on that cute ass of his.

CHEYENNE LOVE

Chapter Twenty-Four

The Solution

They sat down for breakfast and Marc turned to Jamie. "Okay Jamie, what was your brilliant idea that you wanted to tell me?"

"What would you think if I didn't sell the farm?"

Marc started getting nervous and wondered where this conversation was leading. Was Jamie having second thoughts about moving? He knew he shouldn't feel this insecure, but after all the times that they separated before, he couldn't help it. Jamie noticed the change coming over Marc.

"Now don't you start thinking bad things and just listen to my idea."

"Okay, let me hear it."

"What if I keep the farm and see if Keith and Derek might want this to be their home? They could live here for free and raise horses for us. We could have the farm as strictly for breeding horses and your ranch for racing and selling of the horses."

"What do you propose I do about not having a groom for my horses, if Keith is here?"

"You and I can take care of them for a while until we find someone. We could let Keith and Derek live here free, like I said, and pay them a salary to help with the groceries and normal household expenses. Well, what do you think?"

"I don't know? I am not sure what to think. What makes you think that Keith will want to come here to live? He is a Wyoming boy, born and raised."

"That may be, but I can't believe they wouldn't jump at this offer. I'm sorry Marc but I can't see four gay men living under the same roof, so they would have to find a place anyway, and their funds might be tighter that way than what I am proposing. I mean, come on, a free house instead of one they would have to shell out money for? They would be foolish to turn that down, and besides, Keith has always acted like he was comfortable here at the farm and I know Derek loves this farm."

"Well, okay, but what about the main house? What are you going to do with that?"

"I thought we could hire someone to live there and take care of it and we would have a place here of our own when we come to visit Derek and Keith and check on the new foals."

"What kind of people?"

"I thought like a husband and wife team who would stay here, and whenever we come they could be here to take care of us, cooking, etc."

"Wouldn't they need a staff to help them? Maybe a couple could manage the house but they could have a cook and a maid, at least. You and I certainly have the money to maintain three houses."

"That sounds like you're getting on board with this idea." Jamie said with a big smile on his face. Marc couldn't resist that smile; he leaned over and kissed him lightly. "Yes, I am beginning to see how this might work and if we did this, you would be able to keep your place that you love so much, too. That's the best part of your idea, because I know how much this was hurting you."

"Don't think like that Marc, I want to be with you no matter what I have to do to get there. Sell my home or not, but if I can have the best of both worlds, why not?"

"Okay, Jamie, that part is done. Now, how do we convince Derek and Keith? Also, who are you going to get to live in the mansion?"

"Here is my idea on that. I will ask the Hawthorns to move into the house and take care of it. That way Mr. Hawthorn can help Derek with the planting of the crops. I will pay them a salary to maintain things here and then hopefully we can visit often and I can still enjoy my property with the farm and Walker's pond. Remember our first time when you came to bring me Shadow and I took you to the pond? How romantic that was."

"And very hot if I recall" Marc chimed in.

"Yes I do recall, that was your first lesson that I taught you."

"Oh, yes, you surely did. I might need a refresher course, though."

"Oh, you think so, huh?" Jamie said teasingly to Marc.

"Yes, I think we should revisit that before we go home." Marc teased back.

"Home, what a nice sound that has." Jamie said.

Marc was tired of talking and got up from the table and pulled Jamie up into his arms. "I just needed to hug you tight hearing you say that about our home — and it is our home now." He whispered in Jamie's ear as he took possession of his lips. "You know, I don't think I will ever get tired of kissing you. When we get so old and feeble that we can't hardly even stand, I will still need to kiss those wonderful lips of yours."

"Do you know how wonderful that sounds?"

"What part?"

"The old together part." Jamie said and hugged Marc again. "Do you want to call Keith and Derek or how do you want to go about this?" Marc asked.

"I am going to ask the Hawthorns if they can stay here in the farmhouse a little longer, and then you and I go home and talk to Keith and Derek in person."

"Okay, let's get it started. The sooner we do this, the quicker we can get you moved in with me."

Jamie talked with the house staff to get his clothes packed and shipped; he talked to the Hawthorns about staying here at the farm until he had a chance to talk to Derek and Keith. Marc made the flight arrangements to Cheyenne to fly out later that night. When they got on the airplane, they sat planning their life together and both men could not believe this was finally happening.

"Boy, weren't we so stupid to waste all this time that we did, but it's over now and we need to move on. Do you think Derek and Keith will agree to my plan, Marc?"

"I think they will, it's a good deal for them." *I hope they will,* he thought, *because if not, Jamie and I would be right back where we started.*

———

Chase met them at the airport and drove them to the ranch. Keith and Derek were waiting for them and were eager to hear what had happened in Kentucky.

"Keith, how are you doing?" Marc asked.

"I am great and so happy to be alive. Derek told me what a close call I had. He told me that the doctors were not sure I was going to make it most of the time and that's why you called Derek here."

Derek was getting antsy. He wanted to hear what happened. "Well, come on, don't keep us in suspense... What happened with the sale of the farm? I know it was really hard for you, Jamie, but it is the right thing to do." Derek and Keith were both waiting for Jamie to tell them.

"Okay, let's all go into the parlor and get comfortable and we'll let you in on what's happening." Derek went to the fridge and got four beers and gave each one a beer. He then sat down next to Keith. "I am not selling anything," Jamie announced.

"Oh, no, don't tell me that we are doing that dance again. I thought you two were together this time." Derek stated. The look on his face was anger and disappointment.

"Calm down and let me tell you. Marc and I are still together."

"...And we're going to stay that way." Marc chimed in.

"Please, all of you, let me finish. I want to ask the two of you if you would consider moving to the farm? Now, before you answer me, listen to what Marc and I propose." Marc moved closer to Jamie and put his arm around his shoulder showing his support. Jamie went into all the details about both houses. Keith and Derek sat quietly, listening. As Jamie was talking, they both turned to look at each other and tried to think what the other one was thinking. Finally, Jamie was done.

Keith's mind was going in all directions. *I don't want to leave Cheyenne...Why does it have to be this way. Derek was already agreeing to come with me. Will Derek be angry with me if I don't agree to this?* Derek could see the pain in Keith's eyes. He knew that he did not want to leave here. Derek thought, "I will let him make the decision and I'll do whatever he wants."

Keith spoke up first. "You are okay with this Marc?" Marc shook his head 'yes' and said that in his opinion it was a good deal. Derek spoke up then, "Did you guys even take into consideration that Keith would be leaving his home if we do this? Why would you think that it would be any easier for him to leave any more than it was for you leaving the farm, Jamie? Do you think his home is not as important as yours?" It was obvious that Derek was angry.

Keith grabbed Derek's arm and looked at Marc and Jamie. "Well we have all the information and Derek and I will discuss this privately and give you our answer tomorrow." Both men got up and left the room.

"Wow, Marc, I guess I didn't even consider that they would not jump at this offer."

"I think they are in shock and having trouble taking it all in. Let's wait and see what they say tomorrow. If they say no, then we will look at it again and figure out who could take it over so you won't have to sell."

"I love you so much, Marc."

"How about taking me to bed and show me how much you love me." Jamie grabbed Marc's hand and pulled him up to their room.

CHEYENNE LOVE

CHAPTER TWENTY-FIVE

HARD DECISION

Keith and Derek got upstairs and shut the door. "What do you think of this, Derek? Do you want to go back there to live?"

"No, not necessarily. I want you to do what you want to do because I had already planned to live here with you. I can imagine how hard this would be for you since this is your home. It's not so important for me to leave Kentucky because I'm not from there anyway."

"I didn't know that Derek. Where are you from? I can't believe I've never asked you this before. I just figured that you were from Berea, I guess."

"I'm from Indiana. I grew up on a farm there so that's why I know so much about farming, and Jamie taught me about the horses."

Keith walked over to Derek and put his arms around him. "There is so much that we really don't know about each other, but we have a lifetime to explore all of this. I really want to know what you think."

"Well, it would be a lot cheaper if we did this because, like Jamie said, we would live there free and they would pay us a salary on top of that. We certainly aren't going to get a better deal than that. We would have to move from here anyway, because I agree that I can't see four gay men living in the same house. So, we would have to pay rent, utilities and have money for gas to go to and from the ranch. The salary would be the same either way, but we could certainly have more money in Kentucky, since we wouldn't have all the other expenses. That's my two cents! But again, I'll do whatever you want."

"Let me think about it for a while, okay?"

"Sure, take all the time you need."

Keith had so many thoughts going through his head and he was having a hard time even thinking about living somewhere else. Derek told him that he was going downstairs to get a beer. "Do you want me to bring you one?"

"Sure, Derek. I'll take one, too."

"Are you okay, Keith? You look really tired and you know it hasn't been that long since you came home from the hospital. I don't want you stressing out over this decision and making yourself sick."

"I won't, Derek, please don't worry. I'm fine."

Derek went downstairs to get the beer. He thought he would leave Keith alone for a little while. Keith paced the floor trying to decide what to do. He looked in the mirror when he went in to wash his face. *What is my problem?* All of a sudden, it came to him what they should do. It would be so much better financially if they went to Kentucky. *I need to tell Derek what I've decided.* He came down to the kitchen to find Derek. Derek heard Keith come in and turned to look at him. He handed him a beer and told him to sit with him for a moment to just relax.

"Derek, I've come to a decision." Then he just sat back and drank from his beer.

"Well, are you going to keep me in suspense, or...?"

"I think we should try it for financial reasons, but I want to leave the door open to come back here if I'm not happy there."

"Do you think you won't be happy with me?" Derek was a little hurt, but he was trying not to show it. Keith noticed anyway.

"Derek, I'm sorry that you thought I meant I wouldn't be happy with you. I will be happy with you. I'm just not sure I will be happy in Kentucky. I think we should try it. though. I want to tell Jamie that if we are going there, they need to leave his horses with us because I'm not a farmer. I can take care of the horses and you can take care of the fields, since that's what you know. Would that work for you?"

Derek walked over to Keith and said, "That works for me! Do you want to tell Jamie and Marc tonight or in the morning?'

"No, they can wait. I need to rest. Let's go up to our room and start making plans for our future."

CHEYENNE LOVE

CHAPTER TWENTY-SIX

THE BIG MOVE

Marc and Jamie were waiting patiently at breakfast to hear what Keith and Derek were going to do.

"Do you think they'll except my offer to live in Kentucky on the farm, Marc?"

"I think they will, but we'll just have to wait and see what they decide." Keith came down first and told Chase what he and Derek wanted for breakfast.

"Derek will be down in a few minutes."

"What have you guys decided?" Marc asked, because he knew Jamie was dying inch-by-inch having to wait.

"When Derek comes down, then we'll talk to you about it." Both Marc and Jamie felt that Keith was a little bit agitated and that made them very uneasy.

"This is not going to go well I fear," Jamie thought. Marc noticed Jamie's uneasiness and came over to put his arm around him for support. Jamie leaned in and whispered to Marc, "I am not getting good vibes from Keith, and Derek is taking his good ole time getting down here!"

"Don't worry before we know that we have something to worry about." Marc tried to be positive for Jamie. He was getting a little upset with Keith for all the drama and suspense. Derek sauntered into the dining area and sat down next to Keith.

"Well?" Jamie said. "What have you decided?" Jamie directed his question to Keith. Keith took Derek's hand and slowly started to talk.

"Well, we've talked this whole proposition over and have decided to move to Kentucky with some conditions." Keith answered. Jamie visibly relaxed and let out his breath that he was unconsciously holding.

"Well good! You won't be sorry — this is going to be the best for you, financially."

"Not so fast!" Derek said to Jamie. "Keith told you that we have a couple conditions."

Marc spoke up then, "Okay, let's here the conditions." Chase brought Keith and Derek's food in and coffee for everyone. They started talking while they ate.

"First one is, I want an out if I don't like living there. I would like to be free to say if it isn't working out for me."

"Do you mean that you don't think you would like living with Derek in Kentucky?"

"No, I did not say that. It has nothing to do with living with Derek. We love each other and are going to be together, but I've never lived anywhere but Cheyenne and I just need to know that if I am not happy in Kentucky, that we — and I mean *we* — can come back here to Cheyenne." Derek remained quiet and just watched Keith negotiate their lives. He was so proud of him. "God, I love this man and I am so glad that Marc brought him to Kentucky over two years ago," he thought as he watched Keith.

Marc and Jamie looked at each other and then, with just a look, they both came to the same answer. "Okay!" Jamie said, "We can agree to that. What's the second condition?"

Keith took another bite of his food. "Okay, here is the deal. I am not a farmer, I have worked with horses practically my whole life, so we want you to leave your horses at the farm, Jamie, so that I can do what I know and Derek will handle the planting of the crops. In other words, the farm side because he was raised on a farm and that's what he knows."

Marc and Jamie looked at each other again and paused for a moment. "We'll have to talk about this for a few minutes, because we had made arrangements to move most of my horses here. Excuse us, please!" Marc and Jamie left the dining room and went over to the library.

Keith and Derek just smiled at each other. "What do you think they'll say, Derek?"

"I think Jamie will agree to leave the horses there. He'd be crazy to move them if it meant us not taking the offer."

————

"Marc, what do you think?"

"I think we should leave your horses there. Keith will be a good one to run that part of your business. It sounds like Derek wants it that way, too. He agreed with the conditions and maybe he's more comfortable with doing the farming side and letting Keith run the horse breeding. We can also visit as often as you feel necessary."

Jamie walked over to Marc and put his arms around his neck. "Have I told you today how happy I am to be moving here with you and how much I love you?" He gave Marc a small peck on the mouth. "It's also really cool that you're willing to go along with me about keeping my farm."

"I know how much of a sacrifice you're making for me, and I know you love your home as much as I do mine. Besides, you wouldn't be the Jamie I fell in love with if this was easy for you."

"Okay, let's go tell 'em that we agree to their terms." Marc followed Jamie back into the dining room.

"Guys, we agree to both conditions. We need to make this move happen soon, because I have the Hawthorns living there still. How soon can you be packed and ready to go?" Jamie asked.

"We can be ready to go tomorrow."

"Good! Marc and I will fly to Kentucky tonight and you can start driving back in the morning." Marc went to make flight reservations, and Keith and Derek went to pack.

They would be driving Keith's truck back to the farm. They decided to just take what they needed for now and have Jamie and Marc ship the rest to them. Marc made arrangements for one of the ranch hands to take care of the horses for a few days while they were going to be gone. He told Jamie that he would advertise Keith's position when they get back from Kentucky.

The day went by fast. Marc and Jamie flew out to Kentucky at 6 pm. When they got to the farmhouse, Jamie asked the Hawthorns if they could talk with them. They sat down together and told them about their proposition. "I'm wondering if you two would be willing to come to my house and live, permanently? Keith and Derek are coming tomorrow and they will be living here in the farmhouse."

"What do you mean, us living in your house?" Mr. Hawthorn asked.

"What I want to do is have a couple move into my house and maintain it so that when Marc and I come to visit the farm we will have a house to stay in. I will hire you a small staff to help with things, and I will pay you a handsome salary. My thinking is that you would then be here to help Derek with the planting and maintaining the fields."

"It sounds good to us, because we love staying here on the farm. You know I've missed it so much since I sold my farm and moved into the tiny apartment that we have." Mrs. Hawthorn put her arms around her husband's shoulders. "He really has missed it."

"Well, does that mean that you want to do this?"

"Yes! Yes! We'll do it." Mr. Hawthorn grabbed his wife and gave her a big hug. "When should we move in? It's still a little while before we will start planting the fields."

"Move in as soon as you have all your arrangements made."

"We have not really seen much of your house Jamie, so can we come and take a tour later?"

"Sure, we would love for you to do that." Marc and Jamie then went on up to the main house. Hildegard, Betsy and Maurice were almost done packing and getting ready to go to Cheyenne.

"Maurice, make sure that you get Chase to introduce you to your new staff there and get everyone settled in. There's a separate wing at the ranch to accommodate the three of you. Have you got your airline tickets squared away yet?"

"Yes sir, all of that is done. We leave for Cheyenne in the morning. Thank you, sir!" Jamie and Marc were so pleased with the way this move was going. Keith and Derek would be here tomorrow. Maurice, Hildegard and Betsy would be off to Cheyenne tomorrow and the only thing really left to do was to show Mr. and Mrs. Hawthorn around the house. Jamie talked with the Hawthorns and decided to let them hire the cook and the maid. After all, they would be the ones who would be here with them. They should hire whomever they felt comfortable with.

Keith and Derek arrived late in the day. They had left Cheyenne in the middle of the night and drove straight through because they wanted to get to Kentucky and get settled. Marc and Jamie met them at the farm. "Hi, guys! How was the trip?" Jamie asked.

"It was tiring, but good. Have Maurice, Hildegard and Betsy left yet? We'd like to say 'hi' to them and then we'll unload the truck and get settled in." They went up to the main house and said their goodbyes and then came back to start unloading the truck.

"Maurice — John will drive you three to the airport and Chase is going to meet you in Cheyenne. He'll drive you to the house and help get you settled. Jamie and I will be back in a day or so. We have to get everything done here before we can head back."

———•———

The Hawthorns told their landlord they would be leaving. The apartment was furnished, so all they had to pack were their clothes. "We'll move a little at a time until it's done," he told his wife. Jamie and Marc helped them move some, and then went out to the barn to meet with Keith about Jamie's horses. Derek already knew them, but it was just to give Keith a little knowledge about how Jamie's horses are cared for differently than Marc's.

"I'll help him until it's time to plant the fields, then Mr. Hawthorn and I will be busy out there."

Mr. and Mrs. Hawthorn told Jamie that they were sure they knew what needed to be done, and Jamie gave them their first month's wages so they would have money to stock the kitchen the way they wanted. They did the same for Keith and Derek. They felt at this point they were ready to leave all of them to their own devices and they could go home to Cheyenne day after tomorrow. They made those arrangements and then went up to Jamie's room.

"Finally, we're alone." Marc pulled Jamie into his arms. "Are you still okay with this move, Jamie?"

Jamie kissed Marc and rested his head on his shoulder. "I have never been more sure of anything in my life."

"Home. It truly is going to be home with you there with me. I love you so much, Jamie."

"Do you know how good that word 'home' sounds flowing off your lips? You are my home, Marc, and I love you with all my being." They spent most of the night talking and making love.

CHAPTER TWENTY-SEVEN

SETTLING IN

Jamie and Marc helped everyone get settled and decided to go back to Cheyenne later in the day. Marc changed their reservations and took Jamie on a walk down to Walker's Pond. They wanted to reminisce about their first time making love by the pond before they went away. Jamie got real quiet while they were sitting by the water. "What are you thinking about, Jamie? You have a sad look on your face. Are you having second thoughts about leaving here?"

"No, it is just hard to leave this very special place. I have been coming to the pond to think ever since I was pretty young. It'll be strange not having it close by when I need it, but I don't want you to worry. I am not sorry that I made this decision. I still wish you would have told me about Mary a long time ago."

"I know, but I told you my reasons!"

"Speaking of Mary, I would like to spend some time with her when we get home. I haven't had much time with her yet. I want to remedy that today. Is that okay with you, Marc?"

"Sure, we can do that as soon as we get back."

The flight to Cheyenne went fine and Chase was waiting for them. On the drive to the ranch, Chase told Marc that Maurice, Betsy and Hildegard were all settled in and he was very glad not to have the responsibility of the house. He was much happier driving for Marc. When they got to the house Maurice was waiting at the door.

"Hello, sir," he said to Marc.

"Maurice, please call me Marc. I can't stand to hear 'Sir.' We're going to be one big happy family here. Okay?"

"Yes, Sir — I mean, Marc." They all three laughed.

"Where are Hildegard and Betsy?" Jamie asked.

"Oh, they're up in their quarters trying to get settled in. You know how women are, Jamie."

"Yes, I do!"

"I will take your bags up to your rooms."

"Ummm, Maurice, take our bags up to Marc's room. I'll be sleeping in there from now on," Jamie said with a wink to Marc. Marc put his arm around Jamie.

"Yes — he will be by my side forever. I am never letting him get too far from me again. I have waited a very long time for this day to finally be here. Maurice, we're going to go and see my sister in a little while, but can you arrange for Betsy to get us some sandwiches ready first?"

"Sure, Marc." Marc smiled at hearing his name coming from Maurice.

"Jamie, let's go down to the stables while the sandwiches are being made and check on the horses."

"Okay!" They went down and met with the ranch hand who had been taking care of things.

"I need to get a groom hired soon."

"I can do the duties until we get someone. You know I love working with the horses."

"Yes, I know, but you'll have your hands full just making love to me and writing on your novel."

"Oh yeah,? And who said I will be making love to you, Mr. Morgan? Maybe I have other plans." Jamie felt playful because he was so happy!

"Oh, is that so, Mr. Walker?" Marc said as he grabbed Jamie around the waist and pushed him toward the house and pulled him up the stairs to their bedroom. When he got Jamie in and shut the door, he pulled Jamie's shirt over his head and within seconds had Jamie completely undressed. He backed away from him to take in the full view of his love. "I love looking at you, Jamie. I have been mesmerized by the sight of you from the first day we met and I still cannot get enough of you."

"Same here," Jamie said as he started unbuttoning Marc's shirt. When he got it off of him he grabbed the front of Marc's jeans and pulled him in close. He kissed Marc on his ear and whispered, "Make love to me." Marc let out a groan and pulled Jamie to the bed. Jamie lay down and watched as Marc finished getting undressed. He climbed in with Jamie and Jamie immediately pulled him on top. He kissed Marc passionately and explored his mouth with his tongue. Marc was so ready to take Jamie but wanted to go slower. He kissed him down his beautiful body and took each nipple in his mouth, sucking very softly on each. Jamie started moaning and thrusting his hips up toward Marc. He was so hard and ready. Marc loved it when Jamie started moving his hips like he couldn't get close enough. Marc rubbed his cock against Jamie's, causing both of them to almost lose it. Marc put his hands around both of their cocks and started stroking them together up and down, up and down. Both were going wild.

"Marc — if you don't stop..." Marc didn't want Jamie to come until he had him where he could taste him. He took him in and put his tongue on the slit, tasting Jamie's pre-cum.

"God, he tastes wonderful," Marc thought as he went down on him completely to the bottom of the shaft. He grabbed Jamie's balls and fondled them as he moved up and down sucking on Jamie's wonderful cock. Jamie was going crazy. He was squirming and bucking, then yelled out loud!

"Marc! Marc! Oh, god!" as he came in Marc's mouth. Marc took every drop. He loved tasting his love. He knew he would never get tired of his taste. Jamie was coming down and Marc needed to be inside of him. He grabbed the lube and spread Jamie's legs. He put some on his fingers and started in and out of Jamie. Jamie was moaning again with each finger Marc inserted. He pushed his fingers in and out working Jamie, getting him ready for him. Jamie put his legs up on Marc's shoulders and spread wide, Marc entered slowly at first, but then pushed in all the way when Jamie moaned for more.

"Harder Marc — take me harder." That was all Marc

needed to hear from his love. He started pounding him hard and fast. Every time he plunged in deep he was hitting Jamie's prostrate. That would set Jamie off, he was pleading with Marc to fuck him. "Fuck me, Marc…fuck me harder and harder." He kept fucking him hard and hitting his prostrate. "Oh, god! Fuck me!…fuck me…all the way…harder, deeper!" Jamie was going crazy! He was like a crazed animal. The last time Jamie yelled out loud, "FUCK ME HARD! NOW!" Marc grabbed Jamie's ass and plunged two more times to the hilt and came with such force. He groaned, and released all he had inside Jamie.

"I feel you shooting inside of me, deep…Oh, your cum is hitting me deep. Oh, Oh…That was fucking hot! I love that feeling Marc. I love it when you really fuck me hard like that."

"Me too! Me too, Jamie, I love fucking you hard and having you beg me for more." Marc said breathlessly. Marc loved it when Jamie started talking dirty while he plunged deep inside him. Jamie always loved getting fucked in the ass ever since the first time they tried it, and Marc had no problem giving him what he wanted. They lay in each other's arms until both were quiet again.

"I think we should go down and eat the sandwiches Betsy prepared and then go visit with Mary."

"We'll spend as much time with Mary as you want." Jamie started to get up and jump in the shower. "Whoa — where do you think you're going? Did I say you could leave me just now?"

"What? What do you want me to do?" Jamie said as

he reached for Marc's very luscious looking cock. "Is this what you want?" He teased as he stroked up and down.

"You know it is!" Jamie already had Marc hard again. He bent down and licked his shaft up to the tip and back down again, all the while caressing the area between Marc's rectum and his scrotum.

"You love this, don't you!" as he heard Marc's groans getting louder.

"God, Jamie, you are driving me crazy," he said, barely above a whisper. Jamie loved it when he could elicit these sounds from Marc. He knew that their lovemaking was so incredible and was always going to be. It was as if they were made for each other and no one else would ever be able to satisfy them. Jamie moved back up and put his tongue in the slit at the head. Marc let out another moan. "Jamie! Jamie!" was all he could say. Jamie released Marc's cock from his mouth and kissed him on each side of his groin, following the line of hair from the groin to his navel. He kissed him all over his abdomen and chest and then back down to his scrotum. Jamie wanted him so hot that he would beg for release. He kissed him all around his cock and balls without actually taking him into his mouth. "Jamie, you are driving me crazy...please take me in your beautiful mouth." When he did take Marc's hard, engorged cock and balls into his mouth and gently sucked, Marc could take no more and begged Jamie to finish him off.

"Not yet!" Jamie moved to Marc's rectum and rimmed him with his tongue. When he stuck the tip of his tongue inside of Marc, he gasped and cried out, "Please, oh god! Jamie finish me off!" Jamie obliged by swallowing Marc's dick whole and letting Marc fuck his mouth until he gave Jamie what he worked so hard to get. Jamie swallowed all and then licked him clean. Marc pulled Jamie in close and kissed his lips, tasting himself on them.

"Jamie you are *so good* at giving head. I don't think I will ever grow tired of you taking me into your wonderful mouth."

"You don't have to worry...I love the taste of you and *love it* when you start fucking my mouth." Marc pulled Jamie in close and just was content to hold him. They lay quietly again for a little while.

"Marc, can I ask you something?"

"Sure. You know you can ask me anything."

"Can I come inside of you just once. I want to feel what it's like."

"Well, since I have only been with you, I guess I'm willing. I would like to see what it feels like to have you come in me. That way I'll know what you feel. Okay Jamie, anything to please you."

"You know, we'd better get up and go eat or Betsy will never forgive us. We'll pick this conversation up later." They got cleaned up and went down to eat.

"Betsy, tonight we will have steaks for dinner."

"Yes sir. Marc, I love my new kitchen. I will make you a fine meal."

"I'm glad you like it, Betsy, and I'm glad that you all

have agreed to come here with Jamie. It helps to make him feel at home here."

"Jamie, do you want to go see Mary now?"

Chapter Twenty-Eight

A Sister's Love

Marc and Jamie went to see Mary after they ate. Marc told the nurse that she could take a break and go shopping or whatever. He told her that they would probably be with Mary for a couple of hours. They went into Mary's room and sat down on each side of her bed. Jamie could not get over how beautiful she was laying there like she was just sleeping. Jamie took her hand and held it with both of his.

"Hi Mary, I'm Jamie. I hope you remember me. I've come back to see you. I've moved here permanently, so you will be seeing me every day from now on. I would love it if you would wake up and let me see your beautiful eyes. I'm sure they're like Marc's and, you know, I love to look at his all the time. I want you to know that I love your brother so much and I'm going to spend the rest of my life making him happy." Jamie just sat there holding her hand.

"Hey Sis, I am sitting here holding your other hand listening to my love talking to you. Can you believe it? I finally got him to live here with you and me. It was a great struggle, but now that's over," he said as he winked at Jamie. "You know how sad I've been these last couple of years trying to get him here, but that doesn't matter anymore. I finally succeeded. He's here now, so our conversations from now on will be happy ones."

Mary was listening to Jamie and Marc, trapped in her own silent thoughts: *Finally, Marc has found someone to love and love him back. Over the years he's been telling me how he wished he could find someone to love, but since he's gay he never thought he'd find that. I remember right after I fell, he sat beside my bed and told me he was gay. I was not surprised, because I noticed how girls flocked to him — my own friends, too — but I never saw him respond to any of them. I wondered then, but decided to wait until he felt like coming out to me. Then when he met you, Jamie, for the first time he could not stop talking about love. Sometimes I hated you, Jamie, because you kept hurting him. You were always tearing his heart out. I figured you two would never be together and I wished Marc would forget you and find someone else who would want to truly love him. Every time Marc would come to me and talk about you, he would cry and lay his head on my chest. Jamie, I never thought you would come here and I really didn't want you to, especially since you didn't seem to love him the way I felt he should be loved. But now, hearing the love expressed between you, you have my love, too.*

Marc, I wish you could hear my thoughts. You have been such a faithful brother coming here every day to talk with me and share your innermost thoughts. I've held on here because I felt you needed me here to listen to you, but now you don't need me anymore. You have Jamie and

I know you'll be happy with him for the rest of your life. Dad has been calling and waiting for me, so I think it is time for me to go. You will have my love with you forever. I want you to love Jamie — and Jamie, please stay with Marc — for the rest of your lives. Someday we will meet face to face, when I come back for you and Marc.

Mary squeezed both their hands and took her last breath! Marc looked at Jamie and Jamie looked up at Marc. Both noticed that she was no longer breathing. Marc screamed her name and kept shouting, "No! No! Mary! Please don't leave me!" Jamie was also crying. His heart was breaking for Marc, seeing the pain he was in.

Jamie thought sadly, "How can this be happening to him now? After all these years?"

Marc looked up at Jamie. Through his tears he spoke. "Jamie, she squeezed my hand. What do you think that meant?"

"She squeezed mine, too. I think it was her way of telling us that she heard what we said to her. She held on for you because she felt you needed her here, but now that you're happy with me and she knows that I love you and that I will take care of you. She felt free to move on to her new life with God." Jamie reached over and kissed Mary on the cheek and then got up and walked around to Marc. He leaned over and put his arms around Marc's shoulders and kissed him on the cheek. "Do you want to be alone with Mary for a little while, Marc?"

Marc could barely speak, tears running down his face. "Thank you, Jamie. Do you mind?"

"Of course not, I'll go out and let the nurse and caregiver know what's happened. You take all the time you need. I love you, Marc."

Marc once again laid his head on her chest and just let it all out. "Mary, why did you leave me now? Jamie says it was because you knew I'm happy. I want to believe that. I have to believe that."

An hour went by and Marc still had not come out of Mary's room. Jamie decided to leave him alone for now and went to call Derek at the farm and let him and Keith know. Keith got on the phone. "How is Marc doing Jamie?"

"He's very sad and is still in with her."

"Did she ever wake up?"

"No, not exactly. But the strangest thing, she must've been in some kind of conscious state because she squeezed both of our hands before she took her last breath."

"Wow, that is really profound. I know Marc is going to be lost without her. Thank God he has you with him now. He went in everyday to talk with her. He always believed that one day she would wake up. Thanks for calling, Jamie. Derek and I will come back to Cheyenne for the service. Have you made any arrangements yet?"

"No, I'll help Marc with whatever he wants to do."

"We'll see you two sometime tomorrow, okay?"

Marc finally left Mary and went downstairs to find Jamie out at the stables. Jamie had been on the phone talking with Gary to let him know Mary was gone. Gary told him he would be right over and would help make the necessary arrangements. "Alright, Gary. See you in a few." Marc walked up to Jamie and they embraced.

"Jamie, I talked with the nurse and she said that you had talked to both of them. She called the doctor who's been taking care of Mary and me since childhood. He's also been taking care of Mary for the last 18 years since her accident. He's coming to the ranch to do the death certificate. Her nurse will stay until then. I told both of them I would cut them a final check for their services and then some. They both will be moving out tomorrow."

"Do you have a funeral home you want me to call? Gary is coming and we'll take care of any of the arrangements you want us to."

"That would be great. I'm going to have her cremated and her ashes spread on the ranch. She always loved the ranch and riding horses, so it seems only fitting to scatter her ashes along her favorite trail."

Jamie took Marc into his arms and held him tight. Marc started crying again and clung to Jamie. "Let it all out, Marc. I'm here for you — whatever you need." Marc finally pulled himself together and gave Jamie a very loving kiss.

They walked together back to the house. Gary had arrived and met Marc, giving him a long hug. Together they sobbed for their loss, quietly consoling one another. When Dr. Alwood arrived a few minutes later, he went to Mary's room. He actually felt relief for Mary. She was now free of her broken body. He wrote the death certificate and came down to talk with Marc. "I'll call the funeral home to come get her if that's okay with you."

"Yes, I suppose it's time. Jamie was going to call, but that would help, Dr. Alwood." Dr. Alwood walked up to Marc and told him that she was finally home with her Mother and Father. "I am sure she is happy."

"Yes, I know. I am going to have her cremated and spread her ashes on the ranch."

"Oh, that would be exactly what she would've wanted. She always loved it here. Let me know when you are going to have the memorial service and spreading of her ashes."

"We will." The funeral director came and talked with Marc and Jamie. He got his instructions from Marc and then went up to get Mary.

———————

Marc did not sleep much that night. Jamie just held him and let him talk or cry or sleep, which he did all of off and on. He knew Derek and Keith would be here tomorrow, and talking with Keith would probably help him, too. Jamie knew it would take Marc a while to come to terms completely with Mary not being with him anymore. Jamie sent a prayer up to God and asked him to take care of Mary and Marc.

"Jamie, are you awake?" Marc asked.

"Yes, what is it?"

"I thought I heard you talking."

"I was just saying a prayer for Mary."

"Do you think she's happy now, Jamie?"

"Yes I do. I think she's riding her horse again and has her eyes open and a smile on her lovely face. As she gallops with her horse, her raven hair is blowing in the wind.

She's happy, and free of her bed."

"Oh, Jamie, that last statement is so great. I'm so glad you said that because I felt very selfish keeping her here, tied to her bed. Now she's free. I love you even more — if that's possible — for helping me see to this." He cuddled up to Jamie and fell very fast asleep.

Keith and Derek arrived at 1pm the next day and both held Marc, telling him how sorry they were. "It's okay now. Jamie made me see how great this is for Mary. She's no longer a prisoner to her bed. She's riding with the angels."

The funeral director brought Mary's ashes to the house, and Jamie called Dr. Alwood to say they were going to ride out to Mary's favorite place on the ranch at sunset. "We will say a few words and then give Mary her freedom by spreading her ashes."

All gathered at the stables to ride out to that special place. Gary, Keith, Derek, Marc, Jamie and Dr. Alwood rode horses out to the spot. Chase brought Mary's nurse and caregiver, and Hildegard, Betsy and Maurice followed behind the ones on horseback. When they got to the place, prayers were said and Marc talked about his sweet sister. At that point, he and Jamie galloped the horses holding hands and spreading her ashes as they rode. The sun was going down, but as they looked up at the sunset there were streaks of light coming from the heavens down to the trail. At least that was how it looked to all there.

"Goodbye, Mary. I love you," Marc said as he blew a kiss to the heavens.

Cheyenne Love

CHAPTER TWENTY-NINE

HAPPINESS IS LOVE

Five years passed.

Jamie and Marc were sitting on the porch, watching their little 4-year-old playing with her toy horses. "Mary, you know your Uncle Keith and Uncle Derek are coming for a visit today? Do you want to show them what a good rider you are?"

"Oh, can I Daddy Marc? You know I am really good!" Mary was beaming from ear to ear.

"No modesty here!" Jamie said, laughing with Marc. "Don't you think that's for Uncle Keith to say?"

"He *will* say I am the best rider. You know he will."

Marc couldn't get over how much she reminded him of Mary. When he and Jamie found her in the orphanage, she was only 1 year old and she had raven hair like their Mary. They had to make the adoption happen. It was as if Mary guided them to her. These past 3 years had been incredibly fulfilling, their daughter was so perfect and loving. She always called them Daddy Marc and Daddy J. That suited them just fine. Keith and Derek also fell in love with her as soon as they saw her.

Over the years, they had traveled back to Kentucky several times a year and Keith and Derek had visited in Cheyenne even more. Mr. and Mrs. Hawthorn loved to spoil Mary so much each time Marc and Jamie took her back to the farm. They considered themselves her grandparents and she called them 'Nana' and 'Papa.'

"Okay, sweetie, I'll go down and saddle Patches so when they get here we can go to the stables and watch you ride." Jamie taught her to ride when she turned two, so Marc bought her the paint and she named him 'Patches.'

"Can I help you, Daddy J?"

"Sure, sweetheart! Hey, Marc, we'll be back in a little while, okay?"

"I'll have Betsy get things ready for a cookout so we can eat when everyone gets here. Chase has already left for the airport to pick up Keith and Derek." Then Marc took Mary's little face in his hands and said, "Uncle Gary is also coming to watch you ride, Mary." Mary giggled with excitement, and jumped up to hug Marc around the neck. "Oh, I love Uncle Gary so much! He always tells me how beautiful I am!"

———

Jamie let Mary help him by getting the blanket down that went under the saddle, but when she reached for the saddle Jamie stopped her. "Daddy J, I can do it I am a big girl." "Mary you are too little to pick up the saddle. It is way too heavy for you even though you are a big girl, but I will show you how to do it so that when you get a little bigger you'll know what to do. Okay?" Mary stuck her lower lip out and said in a very sad voice, "Okay, Daddy J."

When Gary, Keith and Derek got there, Mary wouldn't let them rest until they all went to the stables to see her ride. She was so cute on Patches, with her little cowgirl outfit and hat. The two proud daddys were snapping pictures left and right.

Marc put his arm around Jamie and hugged him tightly. "Jamie, I can't believe how complete our lives are today." Jamie leaned up and kissed him.

"I thought I couldn't be happier when I came here with you, but now that we have Mary I feel like my heart is bursting with joy."

"You know, every time I look at our Mary I think about Sis when we were that age. She would be so proud of our little one. Karen has done a really good job teaching her."

"Yes, she has. That was a good call on your part, Marc, hiring Karen. She's been a great influence on Mary." They had hired Karen to be Mary's nanny as soon as they brought her home. They felt that they needed her to help teach Mary how a little girl should act and all the social niceties girls need to know which neither of them knew anything about.

When Mary was done showing everyone how great she was — according to her — they all applauded as Jamie helped her off Patches. She was so proud of herself! She was basking in all of the attention she was getting, when Betsy called them to come eat. The barbeque ribs were ready.

"Maurice, gather your staff. We'll all eat together as one big, happy family."

"But sir, I don't think that would be proper." Maurice answered.

"Maurice — my name is Marc, not *sir*, and I think we've been together long enough now that we can sit down at the table and break bread together. Right Jamie?"

"Absolutely, Marc. We are all family and always will be. Now, Maurice, go get Hildegard and the rest." They all drank, ate and talked until darkness fell. Karen announced it was Mary's bedtime, so she said goodnight to everyone. Karen loved her little charge. She was such a joy to teach.

Mary jumped up into Uncle Keith's arms and Derek moved in to hug her together. "Don't you think I am the best rider you have ever seen?"

"Yes, Mary, you certainly are!" They both chimed in.

"I told Daddy Marc that you would say that."

"Can I get a hug too, beautiful girl?"

"Of course, Uncle Gary! I have lots of hugs for you!" She hugged him a long time.

Jamie patted her on the behind. "Okay, little one. You go with Karen and dream of riding Patches until tomorrow." They kissed her and told her they would both be up to tuck her in. Karen took her by the hand and led her into the house.

After giving Karen time to get Mary ready for bed, Marc and Jamie went up to do their nighttime ritual of reading her a story and saying her prayers before tucking her in snuggly. They loved this part of the day, saying sweet dreams to their sweet little Mary.

Happiness Is Love

Keith and Derek had spent the week with Marc and Jamie, but needed to get back to Kentucky. They said their goodbyes and Chase drove them to the airport.

"That was a nice visit. They have the perfect family now, with little Mary. She is such a joy to be around," Keith said with a smile. "But I am ready to get back home, aren't you Derek?"

"You never cease to amaze me, Keith, calling our farm in Kentucky 'home.' I was always worried in the beginning whether you could be happy there. I had convinced myself that we would be moving back to Cheyenne after only a couple of months. Now here it is five years later and we're still there."

"I love our home because we are there together." Keith took Derek in his arms and kissed him passionately. "You better stop that right now or we won't be allowed in the airport!" Chase just shook his head as he watched in the rear view mirror.

"I love you so much, Derek, and I couldn't be happier. The farm is very relaxing and wonderful, and I have never been sorry I made this move with you. I think my favorite place on the farm is Walker's Pond, and I am sure you know why."

"Oh, let me think…could it be the incredible lovemaking we have there almost every day after a hard day's work, or, no — it's the swimming!"

Keith grabbed him again, "Don't make me hurt you," he said jokingly.

Marc and Jamie were finally alone...really alone... after the week of riding with Mary and having fun with Keith and Derek. They always enjoyed their visits but they also loved their total privacy.

Marc pulled Jamie into his arms and took possession of his wonderful lips. He kissed him with so much love and passion that it took Jamie's breath away. He wanted to just melt into him.

Marc pulled back and just took in every feature on Jamie's face. "Jamie, I want you to make love to me." Jamie pulled Marc back into an embrace.

"Marc, I want you so badly." Jamie grabbed his hand and pulled him to the bed. Jamie lay down on top of Marc's muscular body. They made love to each other for hours. Finally they were relaxed in each other's arms. They laid and talked about how they got to this wonderful time in their lives. They talked about the first time they met.

"You scared me Jamie because I had never had anyone affect me like you did from the first site of you. I couldn't stand to be even next to you. You stirred emotions that were very foreign to me."

"Is that why when you kissed me you pushed me away?"

"I didn't know what to do, so I sent you away. But then, I couldn't get you off my mind."

"And now look at us Marc. How happy and fulfilled we are. We were so stupid and let so much time go by that we could have been together."

"My sweet love, that is all water under the bridge. We have had a great life for the past five years that the two years we were so foolish doesn't really matter anymore." Marc pulled Jamie close and kissed him again and again. "I will never get tired of kissing you Jamie."

"I feel the same." They just held on tight to each other, almost afraid to let this special moment go. Marc got really quiet and Jamie wondered what was going on in his mind.

"Marc, where are your thoughts right now?" Jamie saw tears rolling down Marc's cheeks. He wiped them away with his thumbs. He leaned in and whispered into Marc's hair. "You're thinking about Mary aren't you?"

Marc nodded his head. "I miss her so much, Jamie."

"Of course you do. Twins always have an even deeper connection than regular siblings."

"You know little Mary has helped with the loss so much but I still think of Mary almost everyday. Today really got to me when I saw our Mary riding Patches. I could see Mary on her horse at that same age." Jamie just hugged Marc; no words were really needed at this point.

"Boy...Don't Keith and Derek seem to be really happy." Jamie said trying to take Marc's mind off Mary.

"Yes, I am so glad that all worked out with them and living in Kentucky."

"Marc, did you know that they are talking about adopting a little boy? Derek shared that with me this trip."

"No, I didn't know that. I hope they do, because a child just completes your lives, as we surely know. Did you say a boy? Does that mean they have one in mind? Oh my, this is good. That means little Mary would have a playmate when we visit with them and they come here. She would love that. Sometimes I think she seems to be so lonely. Mmm, maybe we should think about adopting another child ourselves."

Jamie smiled at Marc. "I don't think so just yet. Mary keeps us pretty busy."

"Let's go get in the shower and clean up a little." Marc said as he gave Jamie a quick peck on the lips.

Marc opened the shower door and climbed in with Jamie. He moved in right against Jamie's back and pushed up against Jamie's cute ass. "Do you want more, Marc? You are unbelievable."

"Yes, I am and I'm going to spend the rest of my life showing you just how unbelievable." He put his hand on Jamie's back and stroked his muscles and the soft indentation along his spine. He thought lovingly at how amazingly beautiful Jamie's skin was. He soaped Jamie down and then himself.

Marc turned Jamie around and said, "I have a surprise for you, so let's get rinsed and dried off."

"What? What is it?"

"You'll see!" Jamie's curiosity was peaked, wonder what kind of surprise Marc has in store for me? He couldn't imagine what it could be.

When they finally came out of the bathroom in their

robes, Marc took Jamie's hand and led him to the bed. Sitting him down on the side of the bed. Marc told him to stay there as he went over to the bureau and opened the drawer. He turned and walked back to the bed and got down on one knee in front of Jamie.

"Marc what are you doing?"

Marc reached up and took Jamie's face in his hands and pulled him forward to kiss him tenderly. "Jamie Walker, I love you and want to share the rest of my life with you. Will you marry me?"

"What? We can't get married in Wyoming."

"You haven't answered me...Jamie, will you marry me?"

"Of course I will marry you, but how? Where?"

"That doesn't matter right now...we'll find a place that will marry us. I want you to be mine forever and I want to be yours. You came into my life and turned it upside down and then upright again. I don't ever want to be without you. I've waited for you all my life and you are everything to me." He slipped a gold band on Jamie's finger. "This is a symbol of our love. I have one for you to put on me." He handed Jamie the other ring, which was identical to his. Jamie smiled and put the ring on Marc's finger.

About that time, little Mary came bounding into their room and jumped up on the bed beside Jamie. "What are you doing up Mary?" Jamie asked as he hugged her.

"I wasn't sleepy and I am still so excited about today."

"That is fine honey to be excited but you really need to go to sleep." Marc picked her up and kissed her cheek.

Jamie got up and hugged both of them. "I am so happy and I love both of you so much."

Mary smiled her sweet smile and kissed both of them. "I love my two Daddies this much!" She stretched out her arms as far as they would go to demonstrate.

Marc smiled at Jamie. "How did we ever get so lucky?" Karen came looking for Mary and found her in Marc and Jamie's room. "I am so sorry about this, sir. I went to do a final check on her and found her missing from her bed."

"It's okay Karen. She was just too excited to sleep. She's ready now," as Jamie noticed her yawning.

"Goodnight, sweet one" they both said together as Karen took her in her arms to carry her back to bed. Marc pulled Jamie back into his arms, when they were alone again.

"You once told me that you led me through the night when we made love for the first time and I had to lead you through the rest of our lives together. Well, the rest of our life starts now with these rings and the promise of marriage, I promise to love you and take care of you forever."

He kissed Jamie thoroughly, with all the love that was possible for one to give the other. When they broke their kiss, Jamie whispered softly, "I will love you forever, my Cheyenne Love." ☜